Gordon Cubie was born and brought up in the west of Glasgow, Scotland, where he attended Jordanhill College School. He now lives in Bearsden with his wife and two daughters. He has worked in the Scotch whisky industry since 1978.

His first novel, *Unprovable*, was published in 2014.

Scouting for Vengeance is his second novel.

SCOUTING FOR VENGEANCE

GORDON CUBIE

COPYRIGHT

*To Jack, Mary, Phil, Dennis, Rochester and Don
who still make me laugh after all these years.*

GLOSSARY

Bearsden and Milngavie (pronounced Mill-guy) are popular suburban towns situated to the north west of the city of Glasgow. Both are on the railway line into Glasgow and many residents commute into Glasgow to work or study every day.

Drymen (pronounced Drimmin) is a town north of Glasgow where the trunk road splits in two, one fork to Stirling and one to Loch Lomond.

Fort William is a highland town which sits at the southern end of The Great Glen, on the A82 trunk road from Glasgow to Inverness.

The Procurator Fiscal is the Scottish equivalent of the Crown Prosecution Service. They investigate all sudden and suspicious deaths, and decide whether or not to prosecute them.

Midge – a small insect, the bane of all walkers, campers, or anyone pursuing an outdoor activity, principally in the west of Scotland. Usually found in swarms. (Genus – "Wee-flying Bitey-nuisance")

One

Friday 2nd July, 2010

It was the summer of 2010, and the FIFA Football World Cup was taking place in South Africa. Every evening, the teams' and fans' spectacular colours were displayed on television screens all over the world and the word 'vuvuzela' - the loud, exuberant South African horn – had entered the world's vocabulary and consciousness. Scotland had, once again, failed to qualify for the finals, but that didn't stop the Scots fans choosing other teams to support instead. Any excuse to have a drink and to watch football on television.

Scottish schools had broken up for their summer holidays and families were already heading for the airports to fly away to sunnier climes for their annual two weeks of guaranteed clear blue sky and heat – two things that could not be guaranteed at home.

In the service department of a large car showroom in Glasgow, surrounded by a display of lots of shiny new cars, John Lindsay couldn't wait for five-thirty. It was Friday afternoon and he was taking the next two weeks off. He sat working at the reception desk and kept looking up at the clock on the wall, willing it to tick faster, but each movement of the second hand seemed even slower than the one that preceded it. It wasn't that he didn't like his job – he did – but his annual two weeks of holiday were about to start.

He dealt with his last customer at five-twenty. A middle-aged businessman was collecting his car which had been in for its annual service. John explained all the work that had been done on it and the man handed over his credit card to settle the invoice.

John processed the payment for him and gave the man his card and receipt.

"I'll get your car brought round to the door, Mr Anderson," said John. "It'll just take a minute."

He made a quick phone call, and the satisfied customer thanked him and wished him a pleasant weekend.
John grinned happily as he replied, "It's not just the weekend for me. I finish tonight for two weeks holiday."

"Lucky you! Have a good time." The customer saw his car stopping outside the door and he said goodbye.

John had talked of nothing else for weeks. All his preparations and arrangements had been made, and checked. John didn't have a family and wasn't jetting off to somewhere hot. He was going to spend his holiday, on his own, walking The West Highland Way. He had been keeping a careful eye on the weather forecast updates and the conditions looked ideal. There were to be ten days of dry weather and not too hot. Just perfect for walking.

The West Highland Way is a ninety six mile walking route which links Milngavie, just north of Glasgow to the town of Fort William in the Scottish Highlands. It is a challenging walk which passes the famous shores of Loch Lomond, the mountain Ben Lomond, across Rannoch Moor to the head of the historic Glencoe – where, in February 1692, thirty eight members of the Clan MacDonald were massacred because they didn't swear an oath of allegiance to the King, and forty others died of exposure after their homes were destroyed - past Loch Leven and Glen Nevis, finishing at Fort William near the bottom of Ben Nevis, at 4,409 feet above sea level, the highest mountain in the British Isles. Most walkers begin at the southern end as that has a less difficult start before reaching the 'serious stuff'.

The route covers moors, dense woodland, rolling hills and Highland mountains. The walk follows Drover Roads, old military roads, disused railway tracks and footpaths that a mountain goat would find difficult. When the weather is good, the scenery is astounding. Every year, thousands of walkers from all over Scotland, Britain and Europe set off from the stone marker in the centre of Milngavie on their own, in small or large groups and, in the process, raise thousands of pounds for charities through sponsorship.

John Lindsay wasn't intending to raise money, he just enjoyed walking. Over the past few years, he had covered most of the well-known walking routes around Scotland. He had a good pair of walking boots, thick socks and a solid rucksack – all of which had seen a lot of use. There are inns and hotels which welcome walkers all along the route as well as companies who will safely transport your luggage from stage to stage while you walk unencumbered but John was going to carry his lightweight one-man tent, his sleeping bag and his supplies in the rucksack on his back.

In his mid-thirties, he was a very experienced walker and planned to cover roughly fifteen miles per day, stopping to buy supplies of food and water at various places along the route. Most nights, he would have his dinner at one of the wayside inns. When he reached the town of Fort William, he would take the train back down to Glasgow.

He had put all his plans and arrangements onto his Facebook page so that his colleagues and friends, if they chose, could see where he planned to be camping each night. When he got back home, having completed the walk and bought the obligatory 'I Walked The West Highland Way' t-shirt, he would upload all the stunning photographs he intended to take of the lochs, mountains and glens.

For the last few minutes before he finished work, he tidied his desk and put his paper coffee cup in the bin. He chatted with Jacquie, his younger colleague.

"I don't know how you can sleep in a wee tent," said Jacquie. "It's not for me. It would be far too cold - and claustrophobic. And, what about all the midges? They'll be murder up there. And where do you go to the toilet when you're stuck out in the middle of nowhere?"

Her onslaught of questions was never going to persuade John to change his plans.

"It's not cold, especially at this time of year. I've slept in a tent loads of times. The secret is not to put blankets on top of you but underneath. That stops any cold coming up from the ground so you feel warmer. And the midges don't really bother me," said John. "And I'm pitching the tent near enough to civilisation each night. I can use the toilets in the inns where I have my dinner. I'll walk all day and work up an appetite so I'll be ready for a right good meal. I'll manage."

It was now time to go so they said goodnight. "See you in two weeks," said Jacquie, still not convinced by John's answers.

Saturday 3rd July, 2010

John set off on the Saturday morning about nine o'clock. The weather was perfect for walking, exactly as was forecast, and he took a taxi from his house to the car park close to starting point where, like thousands of others, he gave his camera to a passer-by and asked him to take his photo beside the marker stone monument and bench at the start. The East European busker, who was always there on a Saturday, stopped playing his fiddle for a moment and stood aside so that John could get his photograph taken. Once that was done, he set off out of Milngavie and north across the Country Park and Mugdock Moor. He made good time and by late afternoon, he had covered sixteen miles he'd planned which took him through Rob Roy country to just past the town of Drymen, towards Balmaha at the side of Loch Lomond. There would be a fairly steep hill to walk up the next morning.

He stopped at a suitable place to pitch his tent by the side of the track, took the rucksack off his back and started to get the tent out of its holder. It was a modern lightweight tent with a fixed groundsheet and was very easy to put up. This took him a few minutes and he tapped the metal tent pegs into the ground with a small mallet. He unrolled his sleeping bag and put it in the tent with the rest of his things. Once he was organised, he left the tent and walked the short distance into Drymen to get some dinner.

At The Drover's Inn, he washed his hands, and then enjoyed a steak and ale pie with seasonal vegetables and potatoes washed down by two bottles of Belgian beer. There was a big screen television showing that evening's football and there were a few people watching closely while supping their drinks. John watched Spain beat Paraguay 1-0 to progress to the World Cup semi-final and, for a nightcap, he had a ten year old malt whisky which came from the Glengoyne Distillery which was not far away.

It was just over a week since mid-summer's night and the daylight was slowly beginning to fade as he made his way back to his tent. The cloudless sky was a spectacular red colour. John had enjoyed a good meal and the drinks and, after the day's walk and fresh air, he was more than ready for a good night's sleep. He quickly brushed his teeth, zipped the tent shut, got into his sleeping bag, and was asleep in less than ten minutes.

The night was quiet and peaceful. There was just a very light breeze blowing – just enough to keep the midges away. Rabbits and other small animals scurried around the fields. An owl hooted in the trees in the distance. If there were other sounds, John was oblivious to them.

At three o'clock in the morning, while he was still sound asleep, John's tent suddenly burst into flames. It became a fireball, a raging inferno, and, in less than a second, his sleeping bag was completely ablaze. The temperature soared immediately to hundreds of degrees and there was nothing he could do. In his last moment alive, he tried to get out of the sleeping bag but it was useless. The heat was scorching and he yelled in agony. His hair was well alight and the skin on his hands and face was blistering and bursting. He stopped moving as the flames flashed and filled the night sky. They continued to burn for twenty minutes until all that was left of John Lindsay was a charred corpse.

Despite the tranquillity of the night, nobody had seen the blaze or heard John's loud, agonised screams. His body wasn't discovered until the next morning when another walker raised the alarm, after being violently sick at the gruesome black sight he was faced with. The local Police were called out and they soon arrived at the scene. An ambulance quickly made its way out from Glasgow. Everything was a smouldered mess and they couldn't even identify the body. All John's belongings were completely destroyed.

The Police could only assume that a tragic accident had occurred. Had a camping gas stove exploded? Had the victim been drinking and then smoking in his tent? There was a strong smell of paraffin around the ground, mixed with the smell of smoke and they supposed that the walker had this with him and had accidentally set it alight somehow. There was no reason to suspect anything else.

They issued a widespread appeal for any information. John's horrified colleagues at the car showroom on the Monday morning in Glasgow heard the appeal on the television News on the screen that was on in their customer waiting area and, after some discussion, decided to call the Police. They told them that they knew someone who was walking the route on his own and who would probably have been close to that area on Saturday night, but they assured them that John was a very experienced walker and camper who knew all the correct safety precautions very well, so it probably wasn't him.

John Lindsay's parents were also quite sure where their son should have been and they also called the Police who took their details and promised to let them know as soon as they found out anything definite. They couldn't get any answer from John's mobile phone but they tried to convince themselves that there might not be a good signal where he was. They sat beside their telephone, dreading the worst and willing it not to ring with bad news.

The Police search widened and, by that afternoon, there had been no sightings of John Lindsay anywhere on the track. They were forced to put two and two together and had to tell Mr and Mrs Lindsay the news they didn't want to hear that, in all probability, the corpse was John. The Police also took time to look at his Facebook page detailing his planned route. From John's parents, they were able to find out the name of the dental surgery he went to. They got hold of his dental records and these were compared with the corpse. There was now no doubt that the burned out body was that of John Lindsay, a thirty two year old bachelor from the town of Bearsden, near Glasgow. Mr and Mrs Lindsay were, fortunately for them, spared the trauma of having to positively identify their son's burned corpse.

The post-mortem quickly concluded that John had died from severe burns which covered most of his body and it was assumed and concluded that his death was the result of a tragic accident. The BBC Scotland television news, the Scottish Television news, local radio and newspapers all reported on the story. Some other walkers and people from the town of Drymen went and laid bunches of flowers at the side of the track beside the burned grass to mark their respects.

* * * * *

John's colleagues and friends were not the only people who had been looking at his Facebook page. Anyone else who was, in any way, curious or interested could easily look at his page and find out just where he planned to be each night. As he had been unpacking and putting up his tent, he wasn't aware that he was being watched. Eyes looking through a pair of binoculars from a car parked out of sight, some distance away, at the side of the main road, had watched every movement and knew exactly where John would be spending that night. Later, in the fading light, he had been watched, by the same observer, walking back to his tent and getting in.

Just after two thirty in the morning, the driver had got out of his car and opened the boot. He took out two heavy containers filled with paraffin and put them on the ground. As quietly as he could, he closed and locked his car. He waited for a moment to let his eyes become accustomed to the darkness, and then he made his way silently across the field beside the road to John's tent.

He made sure that there was nobody else anywhere near them and he opened the first container. Without a sound, he slowly poured the paraffin all over the tent, down both sides. He emptied the entire container and put it on the ground beside him. He looked around once again and then took a box of matches out of his pocket. Standing back, he lit five of them together and threw them at the tent.

The paraffin and material immediately erupted into flames and, as the top of the tent dissolved in fiery pieces, he threw the contents of the second container over John Lindsay and his sleeping bag. The paraffin burst into flames before it even landed. John didn't stand a chance. He was engulfed by searing hot flames that burned his skin right off. He didn't even see the man standing there.

The attacker stood back and watched with a wry smile of satisfaction. When John's screams died down, he knew that his victim was dead. He picked up the two empty containers and walked back to his car where he put them back in the boot and closed it. He opened the driver's door and got in, started the engine quietly, turned on his side lights and slowly drove away. When he was about half a mile away on the deserted road, he put on his headlights and increased his speed.

He got back home about half past three and made as little noise as possible as he parked his car round the corner from his house and walked silently to his front door. He opened it and went inside. Without putting on any lights, he got ready for bed and went to sleep with a contented look on his face.

He saw the reports on the News about John Lindsay's death which confirmed that, in the absence of any real evidence to the contrary, his death had been the result of a tragic accident.
His plan had worked perfectly. All these people who put their information on Facebook, thinking that only their close friends can see it, seem to forget the power of the internet. Once the details are on there, anyone in the world can have a look. Any interested party can search to see what a person looks like, who their friends are and what they are up to. All the details of John's plans for his walk were there – how far he planned to walk each day, where he was going to spend each night, even where he expected to eat his evening meals.

It was easy for the attacker to find out exactly what he wanted and to check a map to decide the best place to park his car where he could watch from. He could clearly see John setting up his tent and going into Drymen. He could watch him coming back in the fading light and he could wait until the quietest time of the night to carry out his devilish plan.

He'd bought the paraffin weeks ago in small, insignificant amounts so that nobody would remember selling it to him. Very few people still bought paraffin these days but there was an upturn in sales as the summer campers began to buy their supplies. He'd then filled the two large containers and kept them in a safe place until he was ready to strike.

As he sat in his car at the side of the road, a few other motorists passed him but nobody gave him a second glance. It just looked like an empty car abandoned at the side of the road perhaps belonging to someone going for a short walk or who had stopped to go for a pee behind a hedge. Nothing out of the ordinary.

He knew that the paraffin would burst into flames instantly and he knew that the second lot could be thrown at John Lindsay once the protective material of the tent had been burned away. He knew that he could cover John's sleeping bag and roast him to death. He also knew that he could have the satisfaction of standing watching him burn and die and, most important of all, he fully expected to get away with it. From all the news reports, he had done exactly that.

Now he could turn his attention to his next victim …

Two

Thursday 8th July, 2010

It was a pleasant, warm summer night and everything was completely silent. It was the middle of the night in a quiet, residential avenue in Bearsden and everyone was sound asleep. Many of them had enjoyed watching Spain defeat Germany 1-0, earlier that evening, to reach the final of the World Cup for the first time. Over in Madrid, the celebrations were still going on.

In the peaceful avenue, the only light was from the streetlamps and the tiny flashes from some pulsing alarms on the upper walls of the houses. The creatures of the suburban night were on the move. A fox searched for something to eat and a cat hopped silently across a garden. The faint sound of a car or van could be heard on a distant main road. Perhaps it was a late night taxi or a very early milk round starting out?

Then, boom! A deafening explosion filled the air. It was the crunching sound of glass, and the noise of masonry and tiles crashing to the ground. Dust was spreading everywhere in a huge, thick cloud. House and car alarms in all directions were set off by the sudden vibration.

In the surrounding houses, upstairs lights began to go on as anxious and confused neighbours fought sleep to get up out of bed to look out of their windows.

What the hell was that?

Where number 48 First Avenue had stood when everyone went to bed, there was now just rubble, wood, broken glass and debris.

Clouds of dust were billowing for one hundred and fifty yards in every direction. The detached house had ceased to exist. The houses on either side were also damaged with a few broken windows, tiles off the roof, a garden shed destroyed and two cars crumpled with rubble and covered with a thick layer of dust.

Some parts of the house were, strangely, still recognisable. Plasterwork with wallpaper, pieces of carpet, parts of doors, broken furniture and smashed wooden joists could still be seen. The bath was still intact and was lying upside down on the front grass.

What had happened?

Better phone 999.

In no time at all, all the other house lights were all on. People wearing dressing gowns came out of their front doors to see what was going on. Anyone in number 48 was well beyond first aid – if they could even be found under all the wreckage.

It was like a scene from the Clydeside blitz of March 1941 as if a German Luftwaffe bomb had made a direct hit on number 48 and flattened it.

The fire brigade, ambulance and police arrived within minutes. Flashing blue lights lit up the whole road as emergency workers went about their business. The Police kept all the shocked neighbours back from the devastation. The area around number 48 was cordoned off with blue and white police tape.
A church minister and his wife, who lived at the end of the road, opened their door for everyone and started handing out mugs of tea and coffee.

It didn't take long for the media to arrive in force. Television cameras, reporters, photographers and journalists all wanted to find out all about the biggest incident in Bearsden for years. They swarmed around seeking the bloodiest pictures and the best quotes. Shocked neighbours stood on the pavements and gave short comments. The senior fireman also gave his opinions with a few well-chosen words.

The story was relayed to 24 hour television news channels, and to the radio stations and it just managed to catch the morning editions of some of the Scottish newspapers.

The questions began. "Who was inside the property?"

"Mr & Mrs Campbell. Roy and Victoria."

"Did they have any family?"

"No."

"Was their room at the front?"

"Yes."

"Can you smell gas?"

The immediate area was temporarily evacuated in case there was a substantial gas leak. The firefighters worked to ensure that there could be no further collapses of the neighbouring houses and safety engineers from Scottish Gas confirmed that it was safe from the further possibility of explosion, so everybody slowly went back to their homes, some of them inspecting their own damage. Some went back to their beds and some started looking out their house or car insurance policy documents so that they could start their claims in the morning.

Nobody got back to sleep that night. Everyone nervously checked all their own gas appliances to reassure themselves that everything was turned off correctly.

The blue lights continued flashing and rescue workers searched the rubble for Roy and Victoria Campbell. Tall, mobile arc lights were brought in to light up the search area. Heavy lifting equipment arrived and the two bodies were found and removed from the debris just before nine o'clock that morning. Television cameras recorded the covered stretchers being carried to a waiting ambulance.

In the morning, a crowd of neighbours stood on the pavement and looked at where number 48 had been. They were all still shocked that such a thing could happen in their road, and to such nice, friendly people as the Campbells.

"What do you think happened?"

"Maybe there was a leak. Or one of them must have left the gas on when they've gone to bed. It's drifted up right through the house and then something's set it off. Something electric or a spark from somewhere. It's just awful."

The media stayed for most of the day and reported at regular intervals. The BBC, Sky and Scottish Television News all made it their lead story.

2 people were killed and 7 others were hurt as a massive gas explosion flattened a detached house in Bearsden last night.
The couple killed were Roy and Victoria Campbell. He was schoolteacher at Allander Academy in Milngavie. The explosion happened at around four o'clock in the morning when everyone was asleep.

Ian Galbraith, a neighbour, described the blast as being 'like a bomb going off. You could just hear confused screams coming from neighbour's houses'.

The couple, who lived on their own, were found under the debris this morning by fire crews who had worked all through the night. They were taken to hospital but were both dead on arrival.

Four neighbours were also taken to hospital following the explosion, which fire chiefs believe was caused by a leak from a gas appliance.

The Campbell's home in First Avenue was completely destroyed. The next door house was also badly damaged. Its occupants, Mr and Mrs Lee, their son Jack and daughter Susan were taken to hospital.

Another neighbour, a Mrs Kirby, said: "I was in bed and I just heard a huge bang. The whole house shook.'

A spokesman for Strathclyde Fire Service, which sent four engines to the scene, said: 'Firefighters were called to an explosion in a house. There were still a few items burning and there were casualties reported.

'Firefighters brought the fires under control and began searching the rubble and paramedics dealing with casualties with various injuries. The area was cordoned off so that emergency crews could do their work.'

The Incident Commander, Brian Andrew, said that four people had been taken to hospital, one of whom had suffered serious injuries when their window was blown in', while three more were treated at the scene.

He added: 'It was quite a scene. The blast flattened one house and badly damaged another. Debris flew in all directions damaging windows, roofs and parked cars. It was nothing short of a miracle that no other residents were killed by the blast.'

'Crews are continuing their work at the scene to make the immediate area safe and Scottish Gas are in attendance assessing the scene.'

The blast was heard over a mile away but people had no idea what it was.

One person wrote on Twitter: 'My whole house just shook like an explosion gone off.'
And another tweeted: 'What the hell was that? Sounded like an explosion somewhere, the whole house shook and can now hear A LOT of sirens?!'
The Strathclyde Ambulance Service said: 'Critical care has been given to four people following a house explosion in Bearsden. They have been taken to The Western Infirmary and The Southern General Hospital, while three others were treated at the scene.
'Paramedics were at the scene just over 10 minutes after several 999 calls were received at 4.05am.
Injuries include cuts and grazes some of which required stitches as well as people suffering from shock. The next door houses had some windows smashed by the blast.
An exclusion zone is in place while engineers and safety experts begin their investigation into the cause or cause of the explosion.

The experts from Scottish Gas concluded their investigation and reported that gas had been turned on in the kitchen. It spread up through the house and something set it off. The whole place went up. Nobody stood a chance. One of the Campbells must have left the gas turned on before going up to bed. The house was 'open plan'. The dining area and lounge were all one room and the stairs went up from the lounge. There was no door to block the gas from seeping upstairs and throughout the entire house.

Neighbours chatted among themselves. *Were they forgetful? No. Quite the opposite. They were usually well organised and safety conscious. It just shows you how easily these things can happen. It only takes a simple thing like accidentally turning on the gas and that's what can happen.*

* * * * *

The Campbells never knew that, for the past week, someone had been observing their house waiting for his opportunity. The warm

24

summer weather usually meant that people found it too hot and muggy at night and so they opened their bedroom windows hoping for some cool air.

In the middle of every night, a darkly dressed man came and checked the Campbell's house. He was hoping to find that they had accidentally left a downstairs window open as well as the ones upstairs. On the fifth night, they had made that fatal mistake. Mrs Campbell had not noticed that their dining room window was open very slightly. The window blinds were closed and she was tired and forgot to check when she went up to bed.

Standing outside the window, the man slowly eased up the latch with a small screwdriver and pulled the window wide open. He climbed into the house, past the blinds, without a sound and went through to the kitchen. The Campbells didn't seem to have a burglar alarm, or it wasn't switched on, so there was no sudden ringing of a loud siren to waken everyone in the neighbourhood. He had been worried about that but, fortunately for him, he wasn't going to be discovered.

He fully turned on the four rings on the gas cooker and heard the hiss of the escaping gas as it began to fill the room. The door to the lounge and dining room was wide open. There was no hallway and the house's modern 'open plan' design had the staircase going up from the lounge. The man wanted the gas to fill the entire house and this would guarantee it.

He very quickly went back to the dining room and took a small candle out of his pocket. He struck a match, lit the candle and placed it on the table before climbing back out of the window and pushing it shut behind him. He got away from the house as quickly as he could. He was wearing training shoes and broke into a fast run once he was a few houses away. He was quite a distance away when he heard the huge explosion behind him. He continued running back to where he'd parked his car, and drove home.

Three

Stephen and Christine Moffat flew back from Miami into Glasgow International Airport. The plane landed smoothly and taxied to its allotted berth as the cabin staff thanked all the passengers for flying with them, and reminded them to make sure they had all their personal belongings with them when they left the plane.

They were happy, relaxed and tanned. Career driven, young and fit, looking as if they had good jobs with plenty of money, they'd both enjoyed a perfect holiday with lots of hot sunshine, afternoons lying by the hotel pool and taking the occasional swim. The evenings were warm and after dinner they'd gone to a local nightclub to dance, and drink the night away. They'd made friends with a couple from Leicester who'd shared their table in the hotel dining room and they'd promised to keep in touch when they got back home.

The Moffats lifted their bags down from the overhead lockers then stood and waited patiently for their turn to disembark. Families struggled to coax half asleep children out of their seats. As soon as they stepped out the door, they knew they were back in Scotland. For the past two weeks, they had enjoyed temperatures around thirty degrees but, even though it was a summer evening at home, the mercury was just reaching double figures.

They got into the terminal, queued to get through immigration passport control and then went to collect their suitcase from the carousel. Once they'd got it, they went out to find the shuttle bus that would take them back to the long-stay car park. Their car, a metallic blue BMW that exuded money, felt cold inside and they both shivered as they drove out onto the main road. It took a few minutes for the car's heating system to warm them up.

About twenty five minutes later, they swept back into their driveway. Home at last. They got out their keys and opened their front door, having to push a two-week pile of mail from behind it, and put on the lights. Two weeks of sun, heat, swimming, great food and drinks and now it was back to reality.

"Brrrr!" shivered Christine, even though it was summer. "I think we need to put the heating on to take the chill out of the house."

They were both dressed in their holiday clothes which were not really suitable for late at night, back home in Bearsden, and they both laughed at the thought of putting on central heating in July.

Christine opened their suitcase to get a few things out while Stephen had a quick glance at the mail. "These can wait until tomorrow," he decided.

"So can the rest of the unpacking," agreed Christine.

They locked the front door, put out the lights, and went up the stairs to get ready for bed.

Sunday 1st August, 2010

The next morning, Stephen went down to the kitchen to make two mugs of coffee. He looked out of the window at their back garden. *That grass needs cut. How can it grow so much in just two weeks?*

After lunch, Stephen went out to the garden shed, undid the two bolts that held the door and took out their electric lawnmower and the extension cable. He unwrapped it and plugged it in to the socket nearest the back door. He carried the lawnmower to the furthest away part of the lawn and connected the flex to the extension.

His next door neighbor was doing the same, and they chatted for a few minutes about their holidays. They compared sun tans and Stephen moaned about going back to his work the next day.

"Better get on," announced Stephen. "No rest for the wicked. This grass'll not cut itself," he joked.

He grasped the lawnmower handle tightly, pushed the button and pulled the lever to switch it on.

There was a bright flash, sparks and a very loud bang. Two hundred and forty volts went right through the metal handle and up Stephen's arms. His hands were gripped tightly and the whole current went right through him, killing him instantly.

The neighbour, Ian, yelled and Christine came running, screaming out of the house. The neighbour jumped over the dividing fence and yanked the lawnmower flex out of the extension cable, killing the power. They bent over Stephen, at first afraid to touch him. His hands and arms were badly burned and there was an awful smell.

Ian shouted to his wife who had come out of their back door, "Quick! Call an ambulance!" She ran back inside.

Ian tried pressing frantically on Stephen's chest in a vain attempt to revive him but it was useless. Christine was hysterical.

Twenty four hours ago, they were in Miami enjoying the end of their holiday and now her husband was lying dead in their own back garden. This just wasn't possible.

Another neighbour appeared and Ian, quickly taking control of the situation, told him to go and unplug the extension cable and to go to the front of the house to direct the Paramedics round to the back when they arrived.

They could hear the ambulance siren rapidly approaching. It was there in minutes. The two Paramedics grabbed their equipment bag and ran round to the Moffats' back garden. Ian quickly told them what had happened as his wife tried to comfort Christine who was now in a state of shock. Stephen was beyond help. There was nothing the Paramedics could do. They radioed the Police and told them to come quickly which they did.

A male and a female uniformed officer were at the house five minutes later. The male took a statement from Ian while the female tried to talk with Christine. Ian's wife phoned Christine's parents who drove there immediately. They should have been coming to hear all about the holiday but they couldn't believe it when they got the message. They were both distraught and didn't know what to say to their daughter.

Stephen and Christine had only been married for five years and now Stephen had been cruelly snatched away from her in the most dreadful of circumstances. Her whole world had crashed on top of her. What could anyone say?

The Police constable had a look at the lawnmower but his untrained eyes couldn't see anything unusual except for the handle which had melted with the force and heat of the current. *This is a job for the Health and Safety Investigators.*

As the afternoon progressed, the ambulance took Stephen's body away on a covered stretcher. By now, all the other neighbours had heard what had happened and they stood watching from their front windows. Some of the women sobbed. *How could this have happened? What a tragedy! Poor Christine. What can we possibly say to her? What'll she do?*

The Police could get no more information and they took the faulty lawnmower away with them for investigation.

Christine's mother gathered some belongings since they had decided that Christine would come back to theirs as there was no way she could be left on her own. They would have to spend the rest of the day calling relatives and friends to tell them the awful news. They should be hearing holiday stories but now they'd have to start planning a funeral. *This just can't be happening.*

Christine's mother sat beside her in the back seat of the car with her arm around her as they slowly drove away. Her father tried to hide his emotions but he struggled to drive with the sobbing coming from behind him. His poor daughter. His only daughter. He still called her his little girl. Again and again he asked himself, "Why? Why? Why?"

How were they going to tell Stephen's parents? They'd be completely devastated.

* * * * *

One night, while the Moffats had been in Miami enjoying themselves, a dark figure, hidden by the blackness of the night, had approached their house. He had tip-toed round the side to their garden shed and had silently opened the bolts on the door. The shed had not been locked. After all, what was there of any real value? Who was going to steal a spade, a fork or a rake?

He took a small torch out of his pocket and switched it on. He positioned it so that it shone onto the lawnmower. Taking a very small screwdriver out of the same pocket, he started to undo the screws around the casing on the handle. Using a penknife, he scraped the covering off the live and neutral wires and wrapped them around each other then he screwed the casing back together. He then unscrewed the plug and did the same with the same two wires. He replaced the tiny screws and, as far as anyone could see, there was nothing wrong with it.

But, he knew that the first time it was switched on, the whole household current of two hundred and forty volts would go right into the handle.

Safety experts know that a current of this size can do two different things. It can surprise a person and cause them to jump back, getting a fright in the process – but not seriously harm them. However, if a person grabs onto it, they can't jump back. Their grip tightens as an uncontrollable reflex action and the full current continues to hit them with a fatal dose.

The attacker assumed that Stephen Moffat would already be gripping the plastic lawnmower handle and would not be thrown back away from the current. He would continue to grip tightly, the current would pass through the thin plastic layer of the handle and he would take the full force, killing him instantly.

He switched off his torch and stepped out of the shed. He silently slid the bolts back into place and then made his way out onto the pavement. A quick check – still nobody about – and he walked off along the road.

The following week, when he read about Stephen's death in the local newspaper, he knew that his plan had worked perfectly. All his assumptions had been proved correct.

The Health and Safety Executive, whose job is to investigate all serious accidents, took the lawnmower apart and could only see burnt wires since the current had melted the coverings and casing. The wires in the plug were the same. They could only assume, since the lawnmower had been used many times before, that the wires had become loose or damaged. This had caused Stephen to absorb the whole current, resulting in his death from electrocution.

They did not need to instruct the manufacturers to recall all their lawnmowers but they did issue a report recommending that all householders check all their wiring regularly to ensure it is still safe to be used.

Four

Wednesday 4th August, 2010

Paul Thomson casually picked up a newspaper from the stand in the supermarket where he worked. What he saw shocked him and he stared at the headline. *Bearsden man electrocuted by lawnmower.* There was a portrait picture of Stephen Moffat beside the article which described the terrible circumstances of his death.

First John, then Roy and now Stephen. He couldn't believe it. Three out of the four of them killed in tragic accidents. *No. It can't be true!* This was too much of a coincidence. A tent that suddenly burst into flames, a violent gas explosion and then a faulty lawnmower. All in just under a month. *No way! These have to be deliberate. Someone is after us and he's killed three of us so far. And nobody's worked out the link! They look like three completely separate, unrelated incidents.*

A colleague walked towards him. "Are you alright? You look as if you've seen a ghost!"

"What?" said Paul. "No. I, er, no. No. It's nothing," he struggled to reply.

He put the newspaper back on the stand and looked around. Was there anyone watching him? It could be anybody. How would he know? He could be killed any minute. What was he going to do?

He got through the rest of his shift, still looking terrified. His colleagues realised there was something the matter with him but he wouldn't tell any of them what it was. He went home quickly, looking at every passer-by and at every driver on the way. Who was it? Were they watching him? What were they planning to do?

35

He arrived home and paused before opening the door of his flat. Was there someone inside? Were they suddenly going to pounce? He looked behind the door and, once inside, checked every room. There was nobody there. He checked every window to make sure they were all shut tightly and locked. He checked the gas on the cooker. Was there any sign that someone had been in his flat when he was out at work? Was everything switched off that should be? Was there anything hidden under a chair, or the settee? Was there a bomb hidden in a cupboard?

He had never eaten his evening meal in such a nervous state as that night. Had his food been tampered with? Surely the microwaves would destroy anything dodgy. He heated up and ate a lasagne and then had a banana with some ice cream. He was trembling and terrified, and he could hardly bring himself to turn on his television in case it exploded. He put a rubber glove from the kitchen on before he touched a light-switch so that he was insulated from a possible electric shock.

When he finally went to bed, he couldn't sleep. He imagined that every tiny sound he heard was an intruder coming to murder him. He lay shaking under the duvet staring at his bedroom door. He was absolutely terrified.

Should I call the Police? And tell them there's a link with these three accidents. They haven't worked it out yet. Nobody's told them. They think they were just accidents. But I can't tell them everything. What can I do? What am I going to do?

Thursday 5th August, 2010

Paul Thomson decided that he had to tell someone – but not the Police. He looked up the number for the Milngavie and Bearsden Herald, the local weekly newspaper. He rang the number the next morning and, when it was answered, asked if he could speak to a journalist who dealt with crime stories. He was put through to Jack Craig, a thirty year old, be-spectacled reporter who really wanted to work for a big national newspaper reporting on high profile crimes, sitting through notable trials, writing leading articles that people would notice – not writing about a car window being smashed or some youths vandalising one of the local play-parks.

The Herald had a reputation amongst the community as being a focal point for all the local goings-on and gossip but, whenever there was a major local story, they tackled it well and reported it with thorough detail. Although it covered the Milngavie and Bearsden areas, its offices were a few miles away in Kirkintilloch.

"Hi. Jack Craig here. Can I help you?"

Paul Thomson spoke, "Are you a reporter that deals with crime stories?"

"Yes. I usually deal with those."

"I'm not saying who I am but I need to speak to someone. It's about those three accidents that have happened recently. I'm certain they aren't accidents."

"What ones do you mean?" asked Jack Craig suddenly sounding interested,

"The man who died in the tent fire near Drymen, the Bearsden couple in the gas explosion and the man electrocuted by his lawnmower."

Jack Craig thought for a moment. "I know the ones you mean. But they were all accidents. The Police said so."

"The Police haven't worked it out. They've looked at three isolated incidents. They haven't looked back far enough."

"What do you mean?"

"All three men have something in common and the Police don't know!"

"What is it?" asked Jack Craig, sitting forward and taking even more interest, thinking that this could be a really big scoop for him.

"Years ago, all three of them were leaders in the 130th Bearsden Adventure Scouts group. It disbanded seven years ago when the numbers got too low to continue. Roy Campbell was the leader, and John Lindsay and Stephen Moffat were also on the staff. They used to run the group on a Friday night in the old hall in Kirk Road. They used to be part of the official Scouts but, there was some sort of disagreement and they broke away and began operating on their own. They used to run summer camps and had all their own equipment – tents and stuff."

"So, why did it stop?"

"The numbers of boys declined and, in 2003, they decided to pack it in. It wasn't worth their while continuing. I think that some of the boys had left and gone to join an official Scout group and they had hardly any members left."

"And you think these accidents were actually deliberate? That someone killed them all?"

"Yes. It's too much of a coincidence. Three leaders of the same group don't just die in sudden accidents within the same month. There must be something to it. Someone must have killed them and made them look like accidents!"

"And you think the Police have treated them as completely separate incidents since they don't appear to know the link?"

"Yes. They must have!" The caller spoke frantically.

"But, what do you want me to do?" asked Jack Craig.

"Can't you investigate it? Explain the link. Get the Police to look again at what happened."

"But, why tell me? Why don't you tell the Police?"

"I can't!"

"But why not?"
There was a pause. "I just can't!"

Jack Craig thought for a moment. "Ok. I'll have a look back and see what we've got here. I'll see what I can find out. Can I tell the Police?"

"If they find out these were actually deliberate, they can search for the guy who's doing, I mean, who's done it. I want this guy caught- and soon!"

Jack Craig was starting to put two and two together. This guy could have been one of the leaders as well. *But, why can't he tell the Police? What's he afraid of?*

"Were you a leader as well?" he asked.

"I can't say any more," replied the caller. "Please say you'll help."

"Can I call you back?" asked Jack Craig.

"No. Don't call me," replied the frantic voice.

Jack Craig promised that he'd do what he could. They ended the conversation and Jack looked at his notes. Could this be genuine, or was this guy a crank? *I suppose I'd better have a look at the articles that we did.*

Jack Craig dug out copies of the reports they'd published about the three deaths. 4th July - John Lindsay – burned to death in a tent; 8th July - Roy Campbell and his wife – killed in a sudden gas explosion; 1st August - Stephen Moffat – electrocuted by a lawnmower. The Campbell story had been featured on their front page and inside, but the other two had only warranted a short paragraph or two. They all looked like accidents. The Police and the Procurator Fiscal's office had said they were all accidents and they had decided not to follow up any of them.

He also searched Google for anything about the 130th Bearsden Adventure Scouts Group. The Milngavie and Bearsden Herald had publicised some of the coffee mornings they'd held in their hall, and he found a short snippet from 2003 saying that the group was folding. There was nothing with the names of any leaders though. If they weren't attached to the official Scouts, they probably wouldn't have anything about them in their records. Where else could he look?

He thought for a moment and decided that he could ask Stephen Moffat's widow. She would definitely know who all the leaders were, surely. He looked up her address. He told his colleagues that he was going out for an hour or so, and he drove to the Moffat's house. He rang the doorbell and an older lady answered it.

"Hello. I'm looking for Mrs Moffat," he explained.

"If you mean Christine, she's not here. There was a terrible accident. Her husband, Stephen, was killed on Sunday. She's out with her mother. They've gone into town to buy something to wear at the funeral tomorrow. But I'm Mrs Moffat, Stephen's mother," the lady answered.

"I know what happened and I'm very sorry to bother you, and I'm obviously sorry for your recent loss, but I'm hoping that you might be able to help me. I'll only take a moment. My name's Jack Craig. I'm from The Milngavie and Bearsden Herald. I'm just trying to find out something about Stephen."

Mrs Moffat looked rather skeptically at Jack Craig as if she didn't really trust him. "What are you wanting to find out?" she asked.

"A very simple question – that's all - was Stephen a leader in the 130th Bearsden Adventure Scouts back in 2003?"

"Yes. He was," said Mrs Moffat. "He'd been a leader for a few years. Why?"

"And do you remember the names of any of the other leaders at all?"

Mrs Moffat thought for a moment. "Yes, the leader in charge was called Roy Campbell. There was Stephen, a chap called John something. Lindsay. Yes that was it. John Lindsay. He was a few years older than Stephen. And there was another man. Oh, what was his name again?"

"Please try to remember, Mrs Moffat. It might be very important."

Mrs Moffat racked her brain and then said, "Paul Thompson. That was it! Paul Thompson. He was a nice young man. He worked in a supermarket I think. But I don't know which one."

Jack Craig wrote down all the names.

"But, why do you want to know?" asked Mrs Moffat.

Jack Craig decided to tell a white lie. "We were just going to do an article about them, and I wanted to confirm all the names. That was all."

"Oh. I see," said Mrs Moffat, accepting what Jack Craig had said.

"Thank you very much. You've been very helpful. Again, I'm really sorry to have disturbed you."

Mrs Moffat stood at the open front door and watched Jack Craig go back to his car and drive away. She closed the door, still slightly puzzled about what he was wanting.

He drove back to his office, thinking over what he'd been told. *So they were all Scout leaders. And now we know the fourth name on the list. Curiouser and curiouser!* He sat at his desk and decided to call the Police. He found the number for the Milngavie Police Station and he asked to speak to a detective. He explained briefly, to the officer who had answered the phone, and got put through to Detective Sergeant Scott Henderson.

Jack Craig explained who he was and told him that he'd taken a call from someone who said there was a link connecting the three major accidents that had happened in the past month or so. He told DS Henderson that all the men – John Lindsay, Roy Campbell and Stephen Moffat – had all been leaders in the 130th Bearsden Adventure Scouts Group that had stopped operating back in 2003. Did he think this was a coincidence or was it something worth investigating?

"This is obviously news to me, and it certainly needs looking into," said DS Henderson. "I'll discuss it with my superior officers."

"There's one more thing," said Jack Craig.

"What's that?"

"There's a fourth man – and he's absolutely scared out of his wits. He's terrified. I'm sure he's the guy who called me about this. I went and spoke to Stephen Moffat's mother – he was the guy who was electrocuted by his faulty lawnmower - and she confirmed they were all in the Adventure Scouts. The man's name is Paul Thompson but I don't know where he lives. He works, or used to work, in a supermarket but she couldn't remember which one. Perhaps you can find that out."

"Ok. We'll have a look, and I'll get back to you as soon as I can."
He hung up the phone just as his superior officer, Detective Inspector John McColl, walked into the room. The two of them worked well as partners on most of the local investigations. They had already dealt with an attempted murder, two violent assaults, a drowning, and a failed armed robbery that year. There was certainly a lot of variety in their job.

McColl was thirty nine, six years older than Henderson. They looked alike with their 'police haircuts' and dark suits, and were sometimes mistaken for brothers. McColl, his wife Lynne and their two boys, Johnny and Gregor, were not long back from their two week summer holiday in Portugal. Two weeks of sun, blue sky and the boys splashing about in the pool for hours every day. His own sun tan was already beginning to fade back in the Scottish climate.

"What was that? Anything interesting?" asked DI McColl.

"Yes. Actually it was," replied DS Henderson. "That was a reporter from The Milngavie and Bearsden Herald wanting to talk to us about a strange call he got."

"Go on."

"You know the three big, fatal accidents that've happened recently?"

"No. Not really," said DI McColl. "I've been away. Remember? Despite what you might think, I don't make a habit of keeping up to date with all the local incidents while I'm sitting beside a swimming pool with my family, do I? What were they?"

DS Henderson explained what had happened, and said, "He said that they're all linked. The three men were all leaders in the same Scout group. It doesn't run anymore, though. It stopped back in 2003. And, get this, there's a fourth leader. Jack Craig, the reporter, is sure he's the man that phoned him although he wouldn't give his name. He's obviously scared shitless."

"But why would anyone want to kill them?" asked DI McColl.

"No idea," said DS Henderson. "Jack Craig got the name of the fourth man from the mother of the guy who was electrocuted by his lawnmower. She said it's a Paul Thompson but they don't know where he lives – if he's still in this area. He used to work in a supermarket. That's all they could remember – but they don't know which one. It's a bit vague, isn't it?"

"Not half," said DI McColl. "You call the local supermarkets and speak to their managers. Find out where this Paul Thomson works and get an address for him. I'll see what I can find out about this Scout group. Did he tell you which one it was?"

DS Henderson looked at his notes. "The 130th Bearsden group. There was a group that met at the old hall in Kirk Road. I'm sure I remember that a neighbour's boy used to go to it. It stopped a few years ago. He'll be in his early twenties now, I think. I'll see if I can get hold of him."

DS Henderson called his neighbour's mobile phone. He was at work but confirmed that his son, Alan, had attended the 130th Bearsden group, that they had met in Kirk Road in their own hall, and he remembered all four of the leaders reasonably well.

DI McColl looked up the number for the Regional Scout office and gave them a call. He spoke with a member of their staff who remembered the 130th Bearsden group.

He explained that The Bearsden Adventure Scout group had over twenty boys in it but they had broken away from the official Scout Movement around 1999 because there had been some sort of disagreement but he couldn't remember what it had been. All the boys' parents held a meeting, and decided that they wanted them to continue, so they carried on operating as an independent group. They seemed to do quite well. He remembered that they continued with their fundraising and held coffee mornings and jumble sales, and they also organized a couple of successful sponsored walks.

The Regional Office broke all ties with them when they became independent. They couldn't provide them with any resources or insurance, but the boys were still allowed to be awarded official Scout badges for their activities. The group could have used The Scouts Outdoor Centre, in the countryside, several miles north of Glasgow, as a private group, and paid the full price, but they had their own camping equipment and 'did their own thing'.

McColl was also told that they owned their own hall where the meetings were held. They spent their time on Friday nights doing badge work and played badminton, table tennis and five-a-side football. There seems to have been some sort of rumour that, when the numbers drifted away and they had to stop functioning in 2003, they had plenty of money in the bank, all their own camping and games equipment as well as owning the hall. It wasn't clear where this money went. It was believed that they held on to it for a year in case the group re-started. But it seemed that, when they were certain that it wasn't going to, Roy Campbell was thought to have sold the hall and all its contents. Added to the funds they had in the bank, this would have come to at least three hundred thousand pounds. Instead of it being held in a trust, going to charity or being given to the Scout Association, there were rumours at the time that the four leaders split it all among themselves. Nobody seems to know what happened to it. They were independent and responsible to no-one. There were no trustees appointed and the money wasn't audited.

DI McColl thanked him for this information and was told that he could call back anytime if he wanted to ask anything else.

DS Henderson was still working his way through the local supermarkets. He hadn't had any success locating Paul Thompson.

McColl and Henderson decided to have a chat with their superior, DCI McMeekin, to let him know what they had found out.

McMeekin was tall and slim with grey hair. He wore half moon spectacles and looked more like a headmaster than a senior police officer. Like McColl and Henderson, he had worked his way up through the force, and had gained a reputation for being dogged and determined in bringing criminals to justice. Unlike the traditional, hard-nosed Glasgow detectives, all three of them were known for reacting calmly in adversity. They worked methodically and thoroughly and usually got results. They didn't see the point in threatening or shouting unduly at suspects – they just worked their way through their questions until they found out what they wanted to know. They suited each other well and all fitted in to the style of policework that Milngavie and Bearsden had to offer. They worked best by bouncing ideas off each other and McColl and Henderson often viewed their superior as a kindly uncle.

"So," said DCI McMeekin. "We've got three tragic deaths that were all ruled as accidents that we are now being told were probably not accidents. There might be a serial killer in our patch or there might not be. There's a fourth man who might be the next victim and, so far, we can't find him anywhere. And we've got no idea of motive. There might have been some financial irregularities that might have involved one, or all, of the men – but we don't know. Or, there might be something else that we don't know about. And, we haven't got any suspects or witnesses."

"That's about it," said DI McColl. "I don't even know where to start, other than with the local banks. If we can find out their bank details, we might be able to see a large sum or sums being paid in to their accounts back in 2003. But that doesn't really tell us anything, does it?"

"If they got all that money," said DCI McMeekin. "That would give each of them about seventy five thousand pounds. But, did nobody think to ask questions?"

"There are a lot of questions," said DI McColl. "Were Mrs Campbell and Mrs Moffat in on the secret as well? Did they realise what their husbands had done? Perhaps not Mrs Moffat though – I don't think they were married in 2003. Could the money be hidden away somewhere? Did someone find out about it and then blackmail them? Was it enough to kill them all for? Was there a fifth person who decided to get rid of them and keep it all himself? Was he the one who killed them all and made the deaths look like accidents? Is there a team involved?"

DS Henderson added, "Mrs Moffat senior didn't mention any other person. Perhaps they had a treasurer who wasn't a leader? Someone we don't yet know about."

DI McColl went on, "We need to find the old records. Did they keep notes or minutes of staff meetings? Did they keep financial records? Were they that organised? If we could find out the names of some of the parents, we could ask them what they remember about the leaders. Did they have a Parents' Night? Or, an Annual General Meeting? Did all that fall apart when they went out on their own? Did nobody check what they were doing?"

"We need to speak to Stephen Moffat's widow. She might know where any records were kept, and she might remember if he came into a lot or money in 2004. It's worth a try. And there's Scott's neighbour. He might know who some of the other parents were."

"And we don't even know when the Moffat's lawnmower was tampered with, if it was. It could've been any time while they were away. Didn't they lock it away?"

"Alright," said DCI McMeekin. "Go and have a word with Mrs Moffat tomorrow. See if you can find out anything. Of course, if she does know something, she's hardly going to incriminate her late husband, is she? And try to find out as much as you can from your neighbour."

"And, we really need to get hold of this Paul Thompson. If he is a target, we need to get him into Police protection as quickly as possible, and we need to have a long chat with him as well."

"It's been seven years since the group disbanded," said DI McColl. "We don't even know if he still lives or works in the area. If he's to be the next victim, the killer could already be way ahead of us and could be watching him right now and waiting for the moment to strike. We've got to find him, and quick."

The Police checked the Electoral Role for Bearsden and Milngavie. There were three Paul Thompsons listed. They contacted two of them and established they weren't the one they were looking for. There was no answer from the third man.

DI McColl and DS Henderson drove to the third man's address. It was a small, plain looking house in the middle of a terrace. The upstairs curtains were half closed. They rang the doorbell but nobody answered. They had a look around but there was no sign of anyone being at home. It was already quite late so they decided to try again first thing the next morning.

McColl got home around eight-thirty. "You look tired," said his wife, Lynne. "The holiday was supposed to relax and invigorate you. You're beginning to look as if you've never been away."

Five

It was a bright, sunny morning and there wasn't a cloud in the sky when McColl and Henderson drove to the house again. It looked exactly the same as it had the previous night.

"He could be out at work," said DS Henderson. "Or he could be hiding somewhere."

His next door neighbour was at home, and he told them that Paul worked in the Morrison's supermarket at Anniesland, a few miles away, as a supervisor of some sort so he appeared to be the right man. McColl and Henderson drove to the supermarket, parked and went in. After they introduced themselves, the manager, Danny Smith, told them that Paul Thompson had phoned in sick that morning and he gave them his mobile phone number. They called it when they got back to their car. There was no answer.

"Do you think something's happened to him already?" asked DS Henderson. "Or, could he just be ignoring unknown calls to his phone?"

"We need to get hold of him," said DI McColl. "We should probably get someone to keep watch of his house in case he comes back. I'll suggest it to 'Meek'. Of course, he might have gone into hiding, away from the area. Perhaps he could be staying with a friend, or he could be in a hotel under another name. In which case, he's going to be really difficult to find."

* * * * *

Paul Thompson was lying in his bed. The previous evening, after his dinner of sweet and sour chicken with rice, followed by a ripe banana and ice cream, he'd been sitting watching television and had started to feel sick. His mouth had an unpleasant burning sensation and he was also feeling dizzy. His head began to throb. The stress and nerves must have been getting to him. He'd gone upstairs and been sick three times so he'd gone to his fridge to get a bottle of mineral water and had gone straight to bed without even closing his downstairs curtains.

In less than an hour, he'd been sick twice more. He felt terrible. He'd never felt like this before. He'd been sick but never this bad. He looked in his bathroom mirror and didn't even recognise the face looking back at him. Was it brought on by the worry or had he picked up some sickness bug? He couldn't sleep. His head was spinning and his mouth was on fire. He felt his stomach churning. He drank some of the water and that cooled his mouth but just for a few moments.

Oh God. This is just terrible.

He got worse and, at half past eleven, he managed to phone the supermarket where he worked. He left a voicemail message, for the manager to hear in the morning, and said that he'd been really sick and wasn't coming to work that day. He said he'd give them a call later to let them know how long he was going to be off. Then he turned his mobile phone to silent mode and fell back on his bed.

He was utterly exhausted and felt as if he couldn't even move. What could it be? Was he so stressed out that it was making him ill? Could this happen to people? He hadn't eaten anything unusual the day before. Had he caught this off someone else?
He was sick on his bedroom floor as he didn't even have the strength to get up to go through to the bathroom as his limbs became numb. His stomach was really aching and burning. He

tried to drink some more water but he couldn't even lift up the bottle.

What is this? Should I phone for a doctor? Or do I wait until it passes? It might just be a twenty four hour thing.

It wasn't. Paul Thompson's condition deteriorated even more. He felt paralysed but began to shake and have convulsions. His breathing became difficult. His whole body was in agony and he felt himself choking. His entire system began to shut down as his blood stopped circulating.

His spasms soon slowed down and he fell into a coma. He died moments later. It had been a slow and painful death.

* * * * *

The Police decided to force entry into his house to see if they could find a clue as to where he might have gone as their attempts to locate him had proved fruitless. DI McColl, DS Henderson and two uniformed officers arrived and, as soon as they broke open his front door, they could smell the vomit. They looked downstairs and could see nothing unusual but, as they went upstairs, the smell got worse.

His bedroom door was open and they saw him right away.

DI McColl was first to speak. "Oh no! We're too bloody late."

They entered his bedroom and nearly gagged because of the smell. One of the officers, using a handkerchief to avoid leaving fingerprints, opened a window to let some fresh air in as DS Henderson checked Paul Thompson's neck for a pulse.

"He's dead," he told them, shaking his head,

"Oh, this just gets better," said DI McColl with a look of utter frustration on his face. "We'd better get a forensic team in here and call the Doc to find out what's happened to him. I can't see any signs of violence or struggle. It looks as if he's been drugged or poisoned."

They left the room and went downstairs. There were no signs of any intruder. They called DCI McMeekin and told him what they'd found. Then they asked for their forensic colleagues to get there as quickly as possible.

The uniformed officers sealed the house with blue and white tape while DI McColl and DS Henderson went to the next-door neighbours's doors. One was out but the other answered and told them she'd not seen or heard anything unusual.

The Police Pathologist, 'The Doc', arrived just after the forensic team had started their investigations. He estimated the time of death at around midnight and said he'd get the toxicologists to do all their checks as it appeared that Paul Thomson had been poisoned with something.

The forensic team worked all afternoon and evening and confirmed that there was no fingerprint or DNA evidence of another person having been in Paul Thompson's house. They took samples of his vomit for testing and his body was taken away on a covered stretcher in an ambulance.
The Police made the house secure and left a uniformed officer standing outside the perimeter of the blue and white tape. Curious neighbours went up to him and asked what was going on. He wasn't allowed to say anything except that the home owner had been found dead in his bed.

* * * * *

Stephen Moffat's funeral service was held at three o'clock that afternoon at Dalnottar Crematorium, near Clydebank. DI McColl and DS Henderson had already decided to go along – not to attend the service but to watch all the mourners leaving the building. Christine's mother and father led her out, sobbing terribly, and into the funeral director's car. She couldn't bear to stand at the door to speak to people. Mrs and Mrs Moffat, Stephen's parents were next to leave, looking as if they couldn't actually believe where they were.

The other mourners began to file out, shaking hands and speaking to the minister who was standing at the door. There were relatives, neighbours and several colleagues from the firm where Stephen had worked. McColl and Henderson watched them all but saw nothing unusual to arouse their suspicions. After the last car had departed, they drove back to the Police Station.

Six

Over the weekend, the Police toxicology expert, Chris Jones, checked the blood samples taken from Paul Thompson that he'd been sent. He'd been told there was a degree of urgency so he started testing them as soon as he got them. He ran tests for the common poisons that he was used to finding – weedkiller, bleaches, fungi, rat poison and the most common types of drugs. They were all negative, so he expanded his tests looking for some of the rarer poisons which he'd come across before. Everything was negative.

He checked the report he'd been sent. It said that the victim had made a telephone call around eleven-thirty and the pathologist declared the time of death around midnight. There was vomit beside the deceased who also showed some signs of asphyxiation. There were no stomach contents to examine and the vomit tests hadn't shown anything. He could find no signs of any toxin in the deceased's blood.

The Police got hold of Paul Thompson's medical records. He wasn't taking any prescribed medicines except for an occasional antihistamine for his seasonal hay-fever and no drugs were found in his house. The Police also stated that they were not aware of any new drugs being illegally distributed in the area.

The forensic examiner began to think that he was stumped. He just couldn't find anything so he made a call to New Scotland Yard – the headquarters of the Metropolitan Police Service – and asked to be put through to their forensic department. He had a discussion with his equivalent colleague down there and told him what he'd established.

There was a pause before the London expert suggested, "What about aconitine? It causes sickness and signs of asphyxiation but leaves no trace in the victim's blood. It might be that. Did the victim grow a plant called monkshood in his garden? It contains aconite and it's one of the deadliest toxins in the world. It sounds like it could be that."

They ended the call and Chris Jones looked up aconitine in one of his reference books.

Aconitine is an acute toxin derived from the garden plant, Monkshood, (Aconite) Aconitum Napellus, and it is one of the most poisonous substances known. It is an alkaloid toxin, one of the deadliest, potent and formidable poisons in the world. All parts of the monkshood plant are poisonous and it must be handled with great care. Touching it can give a mild dose which can cause an allergic reaction requiring medical treatment.

Aconitine doesn't have to be taken orally, it can be absorbed through the skin. The stem, sap, roots and petals of the monkshood plant can kill if not handled correctly. It is exceedingly toxic and needs to be recognized instantly – by its uniquely shaped blue flowers - and avoided. Many people have been killed deliberately or accidentally by this plant.

Monkshood belongs to the Ranunculaceae family and, in the past, the poison was collected and used to kill mad dogs and wolves, hence it was known as Devil's Helmet, Dogsbane or Wolfsbane. Monkshood has been grown in gardens and greenhouses for hundreds of years and its acute toxicity has been known for centuries. It was even written about in ancient Rome and is believed to have been used to assassinate the Roman Emperor Claudius.

The poison does not have to be taken by mouth. It can be absorbed through the skin. The symptoms of being poisoned by aconite are an unpleasant burning sensation inside the mouth, severe dizziness, headaches and vomiting. If larger quantities are ingested, breathing becomes very difficult, followed by paralysis, convulsions and asphyxiation. The victim writhes in agony and experiences spasms, coma and then death.

The time taken from ingesting to death depends on the quantity of toxin absorbed but is usually an hour. It is a slow and painful death similar to strychnine poisoning. Most instances of contact from monkshood foliage result in irritation, dizziness and nausea. Death normally only happens if the plant is eaten.

There have been cases of domestic pets dying after eating the leaves or stem of the plant, and a well-known Canadian actor who died after accidentally eating the leaves. It has been used in murder cases. An Indian put some in a highly spiced curry and was found guilty of murder.

The plant is illegal in some countries unless the grower has a certified permit. Extraction of the poison is straightforward – one simply crushes the plant in water which then becomes the poison to be administered. Acute poisoning leaves no trace in the blood and the victim appears to have died of asphyxia. It is known as the killer's choice, being ideal for murder.

Chris Jones was now pretty sure that this was the cause of Paul Thompson's death. On the Monday morning, he called DI McColl and suggested that they check the victim's garden for the monkshood flower but warned him that it was extremely toxic and must not be touched under any circumstances.

McColl got a picture of it from the internet and went to Paul Thompson's house. They checked all over his garden as well as those of his immediate neighbours but there was no trace of the deadly plant.

He returned to his office at the Police station. "Well, that was a waste of time," he said to DS Henderson. "So, if it didn't come from his garden, where did it come from? How easily available is this plant?"

"I've looked it up on the internet," said DS Henderson. "You can order seeds very easily but I can't see anything on the sites for the local garden centres saying that they sell it."

"Give them a phone and find out if they do stock it, and if they sell a lot of it," instructed DI McColl.

DS Henderson got the numbers and gave them a call. Neither of them stocked or sold monkshood. They said it was too dangerous to have it on display where members of the public, especially children, were walking about.

"Does it come with a warning?" asked DI McColl. "If anyone can just order it on-line, is there a poison symbol on the packet? Is it a controlled item? If this stuff is as deadly as Chris Jones says it is, why isn't it wiping out half the population?"

"You need to swallow it for it to kill you," said DS Henderson. "According to the internet, if you touch it, you just get a bad rash – but you have to make sure you don't touch your mouth after touching the plant. It said that the Chinese even use tiny amounts in some of their herbal medicines."

"So it looks as if Paul Thompson has eaten some," said DI McColl. "Enough for a fatal dose. Do we know if it has a taste?"

"I don't think so. But, it could have been mixed in with something else he ate. The post mortem couldn't establish what his last meal was as he'd been sick at least once. Possibly more if he was already phoning his work earlier."

"So where could it have come from? And, has our mystery killer struck again?"

*****

Indeed he had.

Less than a year ago, Donald Wilson, a twenty seven year old man had gone into Morrison's supermarket to buy a couple of things. It was not his usual store and he was casually wandering about trying to find the things he was looking for.

He was of medium height and was quite thin. He had short fair hair which looked unwashed and lank. He wore a plain black hooded sweatshirt and black jeans and on his feet he wore an old pair of canvas shoes. He appeared as if he was down on his luck which he usually was. He lived on his own and had never had a girlfriend. He had a job as a sales person for an electrical store and the extra commission he earned when he sold something was a great help. He lived in a small house in a less well off part of Hardgate. His parents had divorced when he was eleven and he'd stayed with his mother rather than his violent, drunken father.

His mother had been a school cleaner and she had smoked her way into an early grave by the time he was twenty four, leaving him alone but with the house. He had a small Nissan car which had had two previous owners. It was starting to show its age but it managed to start every morning to get him to work. He had no savings and usually just managed to get by each month. He was always broke by pay day. Luxuries, even small ones, were out of the question. His shopping was for microwave meals for one. They were usually plain and bland and they had little variety but, every month on pay day, he treated himself to an Indian take-away. He ate half of it and then put it in the fridge to be microwaved the following night.

He was in Morrison's looking to see what he could afford. He was hoping they had some good things on special offer. Then he saw Paul Thompson speaking to a colleague at the store's Customer Service desk.

No! It can't be! This is where the bastard works. His pulse began to race and he could feel beads of sweat forming on his forehead. *Look at him just standing there – Mr High and Mighty - as if butter wouldn't melt in his mouth.*

He stood and stared at him as the terrible memories came flooding back. He had done all he could to forget all about them. He had tried to put them to the back of his mind. He could feel himself shaking. Was it rage or was it fear?

He took his basket to the checkout and paid as quickly as he could so he could get out. He couldn't stop thinking about Paul Thompson all the way home to his flat. *That bastard! That evil, evil bastard!*

He got home and started putting away his purchases intio his kitchen cupboards. He couldn't stop shaking.

Where are my tablets? There must be some left, somewhere?

He was looking for the packet of tranquilisers his doctor had prescribed for him. He'd taken them for years but had finally managed to do without them three months ago. He found the packet in a cupboard and he took one out and swallowed it quickly.

He couldn't sleep that night. He kept seeing Paul Thompson with his supermarket uniform, standing chatting happily with his colleague. Smiling, laughing, not a care in the world, guilt free. *They don't know what he's really like. They don't know what he's capable of. They just think he works there and gets on with his job.*

They don't know that he's just scum that should be punished. Everyone there should get to find out what he's done.

The young man lay in his bed with his mind racing, his head full of Paul Thompson. The next few nights were sleepless or filled with nightmares. His thoughts began to turn towards doing something about it. He knew he couldn't tell anyone. The stress would be too much for him. Would anyone believe him? It had happened years ago and he thought there was no way of proving it.

He made up his mind one night, as he lay thinking, that he would find a way to get his own back, and on all four of them. The other evil faces appeared in his mind. He was sure that he knew where they each lived. He was determined that they would all suffer. They had caused him years of stress, mental anguish, and depression. They had caused him to be ill and to have to take tranquilisers. They had ruined his life for years. He had tried to forget them but he couldn't. He avoided going near where they lived so that he wouldn't be reminded. Until today.

The only way he could be free from the mental torture was to do something. He would make them pay for what they had done. He made up his mind that he was going to kill them all. Once he had made that decision, some of his tension eased and he did manage to get a few hours sleep as the tiredness overtook him, although he did waken up having had a nightmare.

The next day at work, he looked tired and several of his colleagues told him so. He was a sales person in an electrical store. His job was to give advice about anything from kettles or toasters to large screen televisions or washing machines. His target was to sell the more expensive items so that he could get some commission on the sale. Some days, they were busy – at weekends or on bank holidays – and other days were quiet. Fortunately, this was a quiet day as he doubted he would make much of an impression on a potential customer in his half-asleep state.

He got through the day and got back to his flat. After eating his dinner, he switched on his lap-top and began to browse the internet. One of the perks of his job was that he could buy ex-display goods from the store at a very low, discounted price otherwise he couldn't afford the lap-top, microwave or television that he had. Using an on-line telephone directory, he found the home addresses of three of the men, and he checked Google Maps to check where their houses were. There was no address for Paul Thompson so he decided that he'd simply follow him home from Morrison's one day. He could take his car, wait in the car-park and follow him.

Then he started to plan what he was going to do to them. How could he kill them all without getting caught? He didn't have a weapon that he could use apart from a kitchen knife and that would mean going right up to them somewhere and killing them in cold blood, face to face. That might not work and he might make a mess of it and get caught. They all had to look like accidents. Things that he could set up, which would be guaranteed to work, and he could be far away from where and when they happened. Something foolproof but each different so that there wouldn't appear to be a link.

He had a thought and then smiled. *Why not get them back in their own way? John Lindsay used to organise the camp fire – so I could kill him in a fire. Stephen Moffat taught us home safety – so he could be electrocuted. Paul Thomson did the cooking at camp – so he could be poisoned. And, Roy Campbell? He was the leader. He was the one most responsible. He should get something really big.*

He started looking around the internet for possible methods. What was the best way to start a housefire without being found out? How do you electrocute someone without being there? How do you poison somebody?

His immediate thought was rat poison. He could buy that from one of the big DIY stores or a garden centre. *They wouldn't be able to trace it. How does it work? And how do I get him to take it?*

He Googled rat poison and looked at the options it gave. The one he thought was best was called Exterminator.

Exterminator is a professional quality rat poison that guarantees the best results. It contains the maximum strength of Bromadioline, the most powerful and effective rat killer available with a proven track record. Sold in 5kg bags and approved for amateur use. Exterminator is made from high quality grain which makes it attractive to rats and guarantees a high intake. Suitable for indoor and outdoor use. It costs fifteen pounds per bag.

"Alright," he thought. "But how do I get him to swallow it?" He read on.

Rat poison can be made from many different formulations so selecting the best one can be difficult. The internet offers numerous types of poison but they are not all the same and can have varying success rates. Some are made from poor quality ingredients and are imported from the Far East. Exterminator is an anticoagulant, used by professionals, and is the UK's best selling pest control. It has no known resistance and guarantees swift, effective results.

Rat poison acts like wharfarin by causing the blood not to coagulate which leads to organ failure and then death. Humans would have to swallow it in sufficiently large quantities for it to prove fatal and there are antidotes available.

"Perhaps not," he thought. "That's not really practical."

He continued browsing. *What else is there? Here's something – poisonous mushrooms.* He read the article that opened up.

A woman died after eating one of the world's most deadly mushrooms that she had found in her own garden. The woman had not realised that she had gathered poisonous death cap mushrooms and she had used them to make soup for her family. She had found the mushrooms in her garden and ate a large quantity of the soup with her lunch. She began to feel unwell and was later rushed to hospital. She died from multiple organ failure the following day in intensive care. Her husband and sons ate a smaller amount, the coroner heard, and recovered.

The inquest was told that eating just half a death cap mushroom can be fatal and there is no antidote. The husband said that his wife had picked the mushrooms when he was out and he did not know how many she had used in the soup. She might even have eaten more when she was preparing the soup. They taste the same as normal mushrooms. The woman started vomitting and they had called the doctor who thought he had a virus until they told him about the mushroom soup. The doctor reported that she had suffered several cardiac arrests and the toxins struck her liver and kidneys.

With death cap mushrooms, just half a mushroom is enough to kill someone. There are a handful of such deaths every year in the UK. The woman's tragic death was ruled as 'misadventure' at the inquest and the coroner said it was a very tragic case. He said that he suspected that the woman took a considerable amount as the amount of toxins in her system was too great for her to survive. The coroner warned other people to take great care when picking wild mushrooms. The family thanked the hospital for all their efforts to save her.

"Now that looks a lot more promising," he thought. "If I could get hold of some of these death caps, they could do the trick. But where would I get them and how could I get him to eat them? Could I swap poisonous ones for normal ones? He might not even eat normal ones. Would I have to follow him doing his shopping in the hope that he bought some, and then swap them without anybody seeing me? I would have to keep a fresh supply at all times so I could make the swap."

He thought some more. "No, this is impossible. But, could I get some of these death cap mushrooms and crush the poison out of them and then find a way of adding it to some other food he was eating? No. This is all sounding too difficult."

He continued browsing the internet for other types of poison. There were pages about cyanide, arsenic and strychnine and how lethal they are. *That's all very well but where am I supposed to get any of those? What else is there? There must be something that's easier to get hold of and a lot easier to administer.*
Then, he found it. A page about aconitine.

Aconitine is a lethal toxin found in the garden plant, Monkshood, and it is one of the most poisonous substances known to man. It is one of the deadliest and formidable poisons in the world. Every part of the plant is poisonous and it has to be handled with great care. Even touching it can cause an allergic reaction requiring urgent medical treatment.

It doesn't have to be swallowed. It can be absorbed through the skin. Any part of the plant can kill if it is not handled properly. It is highly toxic and many people have been killed deliberately or accidentally by this plant. The symptoms of being poisoned by aconite include a burning sensation in the mouth, severe dizziness, headaches and vomiting. If a large quantity is ingested, breathing becomes difficult, followed by paralysis, convulsions and asphyxiation. The victim will writhe in agony and experiences convulsions, coma and then death.

It has an unusual flavour but it can be consumed without knowing if it is added to food with a strong taste. A lethal dose would be 30-40ml.

Monkshood has been grown in gardens for hundreds of years and its acute toxicity has been known for centuries. The plant is banned in many countries unless the grower has a certified permit.

Extraction of the poison is relatively straightforward – simply crush the plant in water which then becomes the poison to be administered. Acute poisoning leaves no trace in the blood and the victim appears to have died of asphyxia. It is known as the killer's choice, being ideal for murder.

"Ideal for murder. This stuff would be perfect," he thought. He looked up Monkshood and saw pictures of a pleasant looking blue plant. Pretty but deadly. He then found various on-line retailers that were selling the seeds and they didn't cost much. They could be planted in September or October and, by the following summer, he would have an ample supply of deadly poison just waiting to be used. He placed an order for a packet of seeds.

But the next question was how to administer it. Making up the poison seemed to be quite easy. He would wear thick rubber gloves and crush the stem and leaves then mix them in a bowl of water. He thought for a few moments. The same on-line shopping site also had a large selection of hypodermic syringes and even needles. He could get a syringe and fill it with this deadly poison and then inject it into Paul Thompson's food. He could follow him when he was shopping and wait for an opportunity to inject it into an orange, a banana or a tomato. *Some soft fleshy fruit where it wouldn't show. It would only take a second to inject it. He'd know nothing about it, and then, whenever he ate the injected fruit, that would be him. He wouldn't stand a chance.*

He thought it might be better to wait a few weeks before ordering them in case somebody was monitoring his purchases and would think it strange that he was ordering a source of deadly poison at the same time as a selection of syringes.

The seeds arrived within a few days and there were easy instructions to follow.

Plant the seeds in moist soil. The plant grows well in sunlight but likes some shade so do not plant in open spaces. Monkshood likes to grow within shrubs and among other plants. They rarely grow on their own. The soil should be damp but not waterlogged and should have a high consistency of organic material. Plant in the autumn so the seeds can settle before ground frost and cold nights.

Wear gloves and always wash your hands thoroughly after handling Monkshood. Do not plant where children may play. Never touch your mouth after handling Monkshood. Take great care at all times.

He had a small area of garden, that he usually didn't bother about, at the back of his house but he found a good place to plant the seeds. He watered them and put a marker in the ground to show where they were.

A month later, he ordered the syringes and needles which arrived a week later. He put them in a drawer until it was time to use them.

Patience was the key. He would wait for the Monkshood to grow and then he could strike. *That's Paul Thompson taken care of. Now, how do I go about killing the other three?*

Seven

He had already decided that he was going to kill them all in a way that they each deserved. He just didn't know how to go about it. Throughout the autumn and winter, he considered various ideas but ended up rejecting them as too difficult to carry out or too fanciful.

"Where do they go?" he wondered. "What do they do? How can I get them without being caught. On many winter evenings, he sat in front of his lap-top looking for ideas. In the early spring of 2010, he got his first positive idea. He was sitting looking at John Lindsay's Facebook page. He had been looking at it frequently trying to get a suggestion and, one evening, it suddenly appeared. John Lindsay announced to the world that he was going to walk The West Highland Way that summer, during his two week holiday in July.

"That's it," thought Donald Wilson, with an evil smile. "I can wait until he's out in the middle of nowhere, far away from anyone who can help him – and I could set fire to his tent when he's asleep."

Every few days, John Lindsay posted some new information. The dates, his planned schedule – exactly where he expected to be each night. *He couldn't make it any easier. What an idiot!*

"I can drive up to where he's going to be staying, wait until he's sound asleep and it's all quiet, and then pour lots of paraffin all over his tent. Light a match and throw it at the tent. It'll go up in flames right away. Then I can throw more and more paraffin onto the flames. He won't stand a chance. He'll be burned to a crisp in seconds. He won't know what's hit him. It couldn't be easier. It'll just look like a tragic accident. Only I'll know what's really happened."

Facebook became Donald Wilson's friend a second time when he saw that Stephen Moffat and his wife, Christine, were going to Majorca on holiday. "Their home will be empty – but there's probably an alarm." Facebook gave him more help. There were some pictures of his home life posted on the site – including one of him standing in his garden, leaning on his lawnmower. An electric lawnmower. And there was a picture of his garden showing his shed – where he stored the lawnmower.

"Now," thought Donald. "If he is careless enough to leave his shed unlocked, I can get in one night while he's away and adjust the wiring in the lawnmower so that the next time he switches it on – he'll get a full household current right through him. Another seemingly tragic accident just waiting to happen. Aren't some people really careless? And really unlucky?"

"So, what about Roy Campbell, the leader. The one in charge. The one who deserves it most. He was the bastard who led the others along. He deserves to get something spectacular. But, what?"

He searched the internet for causes of accidental deaths but he didn't see anything that looked possible. He widened his search to look at home safety and how accidents can happen in the home. He read about trips and falls, broken ladders, loose carpets on stairs and then about smoke alarms. And then he saw something about carbon monoxide alarms.

"That's it," he exclaimed out loud. "Gas in the house. But not carbon monoxide. Actual gas. The exploding kind. The kind that leaks, fills a house with fumes, a spark sets it off and then – boom! The whole house could blow up. Roy Campbell will be gassed and then crushed under the rubble of his house."

"But, how do I go about blowing up a house?" he wondered. "A gas canister with a rubber tube going in through a window? Far too heavy to carry, and it would get found. That's no use. Or, I could cut the main pipe at the meter outside and lead a rubber pipe from it and in through their letterbox. No. That might get found as well."

His most spectacular plan would need some more thought. There was plenty of time to think about it.

As the months passed by, he watched the Monkshood plant grow in his garden. "It's coming along nicely."

He had also bought two cheap but large canisters with screw tops and had been regularly buying small amounts of paraffin – not many places still sold it but he found a garage and a camping store that did – and he was slowly filling the canisters. John Lindsay's Facebook page was now counting down the days and hours until he was going to set off on his trek.

One evening, Donald Wilson had driven past Stephen Moffat's house, and he saw where the shed was. He just hoped that it was left unlocked. He was sure that he could fix the lawnmower in such a way that it would electrocute Moffat as soon as he switched it on.

He also had a good lock at Roy Campbell's house. The very thought that he was sitting in there, acting the devoted husband, made Donald feel sick. It was a detached house with plenty of space around it. He saw the external box on the house wall and assumed it held the gas meter. That would've been a problem if they didn't actually have gas appliances but it looked as if they did. But, he still wasn't sure how he was going to arrange to fill the house with gas.

That night was a particularly warm one and Donald's house was hot and stuffy. He opened a couple of windows to try to cool the place down a bit.

"Of course," thought Donald. "An open window. If Campbell goes off to sleep and stupidly leaves a window open, I can get in and turn on the gas. It'll fill the whole house and I'll be out and far away by the time it goes up. But, is he that careless? This might take a bit of time. I'll need to wait for some really hot nights and go and check his windows every night in the hope that I can get in to the house."

* * * * *

At the start of June, everything was going according to plan. The Monkshood was flowering in his garden just waiting to give up its deadly toxin. John Lindsay was going to be camped outside Drymen on Saturday the sixth of July. The weather forecast suggested that there would be warm temperatures during the first fortnight in July with some potentially hot muggy nights, and the Moffats were heading for Majorca on Saturday the twentieth of July. Donald Wilson didn't know about Paul Thomson's summer plans but he could be dealt with at any time once the other three were out of the way.

On Saturday the sixth of July, John Lindsay was burned to death. The Campbell's house was blown to bits five days later. The Moffats came back from their holiday on the third of August and he was electrocuted the next day.

Paul Thomson wasn't aware that he was regularly being followed. Two or three times a week, when he finished work, he changed out of his supermarket uniform, picked up a basket and bought a few things that he needed. All at staff discounted prices, of course. He didn't notice that, one day, when he put his basket down to stretch to try to reach for something at the very back of a shelf, a man

74

wearing a black hooded sweatshirt quickly bent down beside his basket.

He never noticed that the man had a hypodermic syringe in his hand and had injected a quantity of liquid into one of the bananas in his basket. It had only taken seconds. The man then walked away and left the supermarket without buying anything. Paul Thomson had managed to reach the tin at the back of the shelf and he put it in his basket, had picked up another two items and had then paid for his purchases. He put them on the back seat of his car and then he drove home.

He put the things away when he got home and started to make his dinner. He stayed in watching television that night. The next morning, he picked up the newspaper in the supermarket and read about Stephen Moffat being electrocuted in his back garden, and started to panic.

The next day, he'd contacted Jack Craig and then, unknowingly, had eaten the deadly, poisoned banana with his evening meal.

Eight

DCI McMeekin's office was at the front of the building and the sun had just reached a point where it shone directly in his window, reflecting off his computer screen and his desk. He stood up and closed the blinds, shading the room, and he held a 'council of war' with his two detectives as they reviewed the case so far.

"Right. We've now got five deaths which were all supposed to look like accidents, but we now know that the victims were linked through this Scout group. You need to get names and addresses of all the members, you need to find out if there was any truth to these rumours about financial irregularities and, if so, find out what happened to the money. Did any of the parents have a grudge against the leaders? Did someone not get their share of the money, perhaps? The boys will all be at least seven years older now but they should still be attached to this area. Do any of them have a serious grudge against their old leaders? Why was Mrs Campbell killed as well as her husband? Was she involved, too? Or, did the killer not realise she would be there?"

McColl and Henderson were noting this all down.

McMeekin continued, "Did anyone see a stranger hanging about near the West Highland Way? What caused the gas leak in the Campbell's house? Can you get any more details from the investigation? Was anyone seen acting suspiciously near the Moffat's house? And, you need to get forensics to go through all Paul Thompson's food in his cupboards and in his bin. Find out what poisoned him, if anything, and where it came from. Go to Morrison's and speak to the Manager. Was anyone hanging about, acting suspiciously? Got all that?"

"Yes," they said together, realising that they were going to be very busy over the next few days.

"Right. Off you go. And keep me up to date with anything you find."

They left McMeekin's office and went back to their desks.

"Ok," said DI McColl. "Where to first?"

"I said I'd get back to Jack Craig at The Milngavie & Bearsden Herald," said DS Henderson. "I said I'd tell him what was happening. But, could he print an appeal for ex-members of the Scout group to contact the paper? He might be able to get us a list of names and addresses without it looking like we're the ones asking. Some of the ex-members or their families might see a notice in the paper."

"Alright," said DI McColl. "But I think we should also be working on our own list. What about that neighbour of yours. Let's ask him for some names."

DS Henderson rang Jack Craig's direct number. He was at his desk and answered the phone as soon as it rang.

"Jack Craig," he said.

"Hi, it's Detective Sergeant Henderson, Milngavie Police, here."

"Oh. Hello," replied Jack Craig, picking up his pen. "Have you found out anything?"

"Yes. But it's not good news," said DS Henderson. "We found the address of Paul Thompson, the fourth man, but we were too late. We got no answer at his house, and he'd phoned in sick to his work, so we broke down his door. Found him dead in his bed. Apparently he'd been poisoned."

"I see. So, now what?" asked Jack Craig.

"Well, we were hoping you might be able to help us."

"Me? How?"

"Could your paper print something asking for names and addresses for ex-members of the 130th Bearsden Scout Group. We'll be checking ourselves, but you could help as well. It might not arouse suspicion if you were asking, rather than the Police, if you see what I mean? Perhaps a reunion or something like that. At the moment, our killer thinks he's got away with these 'accidents'. He won't even suspect that we're looking into them."

"I see," replied Jack Craig. "I'm sure we could run something in our next edition."

"Can you set up a private post box or a website so they can put their details on it?" asked DS Henderson.

"Ok. I'll see what I can do. I'll let you know if I get some results."

"Thanks a lot. Hopefully, we'll talk again soon."

DS Henderson hung up, and then called his neighbour, Pete McNeil. After they had exchanged pleasantries, he asked him, "Do you remember I was asking you about the 130th Bearsden Scouts?"

"Yes, of course," he replied.

"Well, I need to ask you some more, and this is official Police business. Would you and Alan be able to come up with a list of as many names, and even the addresses, of boys who were in the group? As many as you can remember. We can then ask them if they, in turn, can remember even more so that we can get as complete a list as possible."

"Well, I can try. But, it was over seven years ago."

"I know," replied DS Henderson. "What about other neighbours? Were there any other families round about who could help you with this?"

"I think there were. Am I allowed to say what it's about?"

"Not at the moment. If anyone asks, just make something up. We've got the local paper asking for names for a non-existant reunion so we'll see what comes in from that. As soon as you get some names, let me know."

"Ok. I'll see what I can do."

"Thanks. I wouldn't ask if it wasn't important." DS Henderson ended the call.

At the same time, DI McColl was asking the forensic team to check all the food packing and tins that were found at Paul Thompson's house and in his bin outside. "See if you can find any traces of this aconitine poison in anything he ate."

Then he got the number for the Scottish Gas investigators and asked for a full copy of their findings. "Where did the leak come from, and could it have been caused deliberately? I need a copy of everything you've got, as soon as possible. Thanks."

"Right," said DI McColl to his younger colleague. "Let's go and speak to Mrs Moffat."

The sun was shining brightly, and there wasn't a cloud in the sky, as they drove to the Moffat's house. It was located in a fairly new development and it was one of the larger houses with a mono-blocked two car driveway. It looked expensive and the detectives realised that the Moffats obviously had money.

It was only a few days since Stephen's funeral had taken place, and Christine Moffat was still off work. Her boss told her to take as long as she needed. The company had a bereavement leave policy for its staff, but what had happened was beyond anything they had ever experienced. She was at home and still in a state of disbelief. When McColl and Henderson rang the doorbell, Christine's mother answered.

They introduced themselves and asked if they could speak to Christine. They told her mother that the reporter, Jack Craig, who had spoken with Stephen's mother, had given them some information and they were wanting to ask Christine a couple of questions.

"It's the Police," said Christine's mother, turning her head slightly towards the lounge.

"What do they want?" asked a puzzled voice.

"They want to ask you about Stephen's involvement with the Scouts. Do you want to speak to them?"

"Yes, I suppose so," she replied, nervously.

Christine's mother invited the two detectives in and led them into the lounge. They solemnly introduced themselves to Christine and offered her their deepest sympathies. Her eyes and face told them immediately that she had been crying – a lot. She looked worn out since she hadn't slept properly for over a week. A half-drunk cup of tea sat on a small table in front of her.

The detectives glanced around the room. It was well designed and filled with expensive looking, modern furniture. The Moffats both had good careers and had spent plenty of money on their home.

"We're really sorry to bother you at this time, but we have some questions we need to ask you," said DI McColl.

"What about?" asked Christine. "Something about the Scouts, Mum said. What is it?"

"Well," said DI McColl. "We know that Stephen was a leader in the 130th Bearsden Scout Group and that it was run as an independent group, separate from the official Scout Movement. We know who the other three leaders were – but we want to know if there was anyone else involved, like a treasurer, or a parent perhaps, who wasn't one of the leaders."

Christine thought for a moment. "No, I'm sure there wasn't anyone like that. Roy Campbell looked after all the funds and the banking stuff, I think. When they raised funds, I'm sure he was the one who counted it all and took it to the bank. They had an account for paying bills and things like that. It was with one of the banks at Bearsden Cross, I think."

She went on, "Roy Campbell and his wife were the couple killed in that house explosion last month. Stephen was at their funeral … just before we went on holiday." She burst into tears at the thought of her last days with Stephen. Her mother, sitting beside her, put an arm around her.

DI McColl said, "We know. I'm very sorry. I didn't mean to …"

Christine settled down after a minute. "Why are you asking? Is this to do with the explosion?"

"Not directly," said DI McColl. "Now, I'm really sorry but we need to ask a rather sensitive question." He paused and then asked, "When the group stopped meeting, the Scout Hall and all their equipment – their camping stuff and games and so on – were sold. We reckon, they would have got about three hundred thousand pounds. Do you have any idea what happened to that money?"

Christine looked astonished and puzzled. "No," she said. "I've no idea."

"I need to ask, I'm afraid," said DI McColl. "But, was there any way that this was divided among the leaders?"

"What?" asked Christine's mother in a highly indignant voice. "You can't be serious. What sort of question is that to ask?"

"As I said, it's important, and we really need to ask it," said DI McColl. "I can only apologise for having to ask it at this sensitive time, but I have to ask."

"Well, I can tell you right now that Stephen had nothing to do with that!" said Christine. "He never got any of that money. We just presumed that Roy Campbell had it in an account somewhere in case the group ever got started again and they needed to buy a new hall and stuff."

"Ok," said DI McColl. "Now, do you know if there were any records kept? Of the accounts or lists of the boys names and addresses, or anything like that?"

"There must have been stuff like that," said Christine. "But, Roy Campbell would have had all those things. It must have all been destroyed in his house. Is that why you're looking for it?"

"In a way," said DI McColl. "So you've got no old paperwork at all?"

"No," said Christine. "It was all thrown out years ago."

DI McColl and DS Henderson looked at each other and decided that there was nothing else to ask. They stood up and once again apologised for disturbing them. Christine's mother showed them out.

They got back to their car and DI McColl said, "Well, she seemed genuine enough. They've not seen that money. Let's go down to Morrison's now."

The drive from Bearsden to Anniesland, to the Morrison's store took a few minutes. McColl and Henderson went in and asked for the Manager that they'd spoken to a few days previously. Danny Smith came to meet them and took them to his office.

"We asked you last week about Paul Thompson, one of your employees," said DI McColl. "We came here looking for him and you told us his address and phone number."

"Paul's a supervisor in the store," said the Manager. "He's worked here for nearly ten years. He deals with the staff, he makes sure that there are no empty shelves that need filling up, and he answers customer questions. As I told you, he's off sick at the moment. He left a message for me on Thursday night. I've not heard from him since, and I've tried phoning him several times."

"I'm afraid I've got some bad news for you," said DI McColl. "We were looking for him as we'd been alerted to something. We couldn't get an answer from him so we broke into his house on Friday and found him dead."

Danny Smith gasped, obviously very shocked. "What happened?"
"Our toxicologist established that Mr Thompson's been poisoned. He must have been starting to feel the effects when he phoned you. He died soon afterwards, in a particularly horrible way."

"Oh God! How awful."

"So, we need to ask you if anyone had anything against him. Did anyone have a grudge against him? Were you aware of anyone in the store acting suspiciously?"

"No. Not at all," said Danny Smith. "Paul was a popular person. Although he was their Supervisor, all the staff got on with him. They all liked him and felt they could ask him anything. Oh God. I'll need to tell them all what's happened to him."

"Could he have come into contact with any poisonous substance here in the store?" asked DI McColl. "Any foods that you don't normally sell? Or something that had gone off?"

"No," said Danny Smith. "I'm certain that couldn't have happened. We do have very high food safety standards here, you know. We don't sell anything suspicious."

"Sorry, I didn't mean it to sound like that," said DI McColl. "When you do speak to the rest of the staff, if anyone knows anything, even if it sounds really trivial, can you let us know?" DI McColl gave Danny Smith his card.

"Yes. Of course," said Danny Smith, still trying to come to terms with what he'd just been told.

McColl and Henderson left him and went back to their car.

"I think we now need to go and see the banks at Bearsden Cross."

There were three banks at Bearsden Cross. McColl and Henderson drove their car into The Glebe Car Park and walked up the road to the branch of Lloyds TSB Bank. They spoke to the manager who checked his records but had no account belonging to the Scout

Group. They thanked him and walked round the corner to The Clydesdale Bank. They got the same story there.

They walked round to The Bank of Scotland on Roman Road, asked for the manager and explained what they were looking for.

"Yes," he said. "I know the Scout group. My son was a member years ago. They certainly had their account here. Let me have a look."

McColl and Henderson nodded to each other. Success at last.

The manager, Mr Reid, took them into his office and offered them a seat. He excused himself and went and asked one of his staff to find the appropriate account details.

The teller found the account number and gave it to Mr Reid. He rejoined McColl and Henderson in his office. He sat down and typed the account details into his desk-top computer. The account flashed onto the screen in seconds.

"Here we are," said Mr Reid. "What exactly are you looking for?"

"We need a printout of the account since 2003," said DI McColl. "There should have been a large amount paid in about that time. We need to know if it's still there. If not, what happened to it? And, we need a list of the signatories for the account."

The manager looked at the screen. "I can give you a print of this. There was over three hundred thousand pounds paid in, back in May 2004. It stayed there for a few months and then it was all withdrawn in October 2004. It was electronically transferred to another bank somewhere, according to this. Perhaps they moved it into a higher interest account since they knew it wasn't going to be used in the near future. According to this, all the leaders were signatories for cheques and so on – but Roy Campbell seems to have set up an on-line banking facility that only needed one person, with all the passwords and so on, to be able to use. "

"Can you give us the bank and account number it went to?" asked DI McColl.

"I'd need to check back the records for that year. That might take a while. I'll be able to get you all the details though. Can I contact you or do you want to come back?"

"If you could call us as soon as you have the details," said DI McColl, giving him a card with his phone number on it. "It's very important so could you give it top priority please?"

"Sure. Of course," said Mr Reid. "I'll let you know as soon as possible."

McColl and Henderson thanked him, stood up, shook his hand, and were about to go when McColl said, "You said that your son was a member. We're also trying to put a list together of all ex-members of the group. Would he be able to give us a list of all the names he can remember?"

"I think so," said Mr Reid. "He's at Stirling University but I can call him tonight and ask him."

"If you could, that would be really helpful as well," said DI McColl. "Let us know as soon as you have something."

They left the bank and went back to the Police Station.

"Ok," said DI McColl to his colleague. "We've got the bank manager's son getting a list of names, you're going to speak to your neighbour tonight, and we've got the Milngavie and Bearsden Herald asking as well. Is there anyone else we can ask?"

"I guess the list will expand as we ask more people on it," replied DS Henderson.

* * * * *

That evening, DS Henderson went to his neighbour, Pete McNeil's door and rang the bell.

Pete McNeil answered it and invited him in. "So, what's this big mystery then?"

"Well, at the moment," explained Scott Henderson. "We're trying to put together a list of as many of the ex-members of the Scout group as we can. And, of course, if we can also get current addresses – so much the better."

"You're obviously not planning a big reunion of ex-members, so you must want these for something, mustn't you? I saw the story in the paper and on The News about that Roy Campbell's house blowing up. Is it to do with that? Do you think that one of the boys had it in for him and had something to do with it?"

"I can't really tell you that," said Scott Henderson.

"Oh, come on Scott," said Peter McNeil. "I'm not daft. The ex-leader of the Scouts gets blown to bits and then you phone me to ask for as many names of boys as I can remember."

"Between you and me," said Scott. "It's not just Roy Campbell. In the last month, all four of the leaders have died in supposed accidents. It's all too much of a coincidence so we're obviously investigating them. So far, we've got nothing to go on so we need to start with a list of names. If four leaders are killed, it does tend to suggest that it's one of the boys, or someone in their families, who's likely to be a suspect. But they were leaders for years and a lot of boys went through the group, and they'll all be adults now."

Peter McNeil picked up a sheet of paper and handed it to Scott Henderson. "Here you are. Alan and I have managed to get about twenty names and a few addresses since the families still live quite close to here."

"Great. This is just what we want. We can start checking who was where. Some of them might have been away on holiday or can account for their whereabouts. We can work through this and ask each of them if they can add any more names."

"You know," said Pete. "I hate speaking ill of the dead and all that - but I never really liked that Roy Campbell. He always seemed a bit creepy."

"How do you mean?" asked Scott.

"There was just something about him I didn't like. I can't really say what it was. But, I guess, he gave up his free time to run the group and all their activities, and he took a couple of weeks in the summer holidays to organize a camp. They took the boys away to the seaside and they had all their own tents and stuff. So, good for him. The Campbells didn't have any family. He just devoted his life to the Scouts. But, he just seemed a bit funny sometimes. I don't know what any other parents thought."

Scott Henderson made a mental note to ask the other parents what they thought about Roy Campbell. Then he thanked Pete McNeil for his help and got up to leave.

"I'll leave you in peace," he said. "Thanks again."

Pete McNeil saw him to the front door and said goodbye.

Nine

The following morning was another bright day. DI McColl finished his breakfast, put his jacket over his arm, and kissed his wife, Lynne, goodbye. She was taking the boys to buy stuff for going back to school the following Monday. As always, the holidays had come and gone all too quickly. Their older son, Johnny was going to be starting secondary school and the thought of it made Lynne feel old.

At the Police Station, Mr Reid, the bank manager called in, on his way to work, and gave McColl and Henderson the list that his son had remembered. Some of the names were the same as Pete McNeil's list but there were a few new ones on it.

"I've also managed to find out about the money," he said. "In October 2004, the sum of £304,710.20 was transferred from our bank to an account at a branch of Santander Bank in Byres Road. Here are the account details." He gave them another piece of paper. "They should be able to tell you the name of the account holder."

"This is very helpful, Mr Reid," said DI McColl. "Thank you very much. We'll go and pay them a visit this morning."

Mr Reid bade them farewell and turned to go. "No bother," he said as he left them.

"They'll not be open yet," said DI McColl to DS Henderson, looking at the clock on the wall. "But, by the time we drive down to Byres Road, we should be able to see someone."

They got up and went out to their car. It only took twenty minutes for them to get to Byres Road in Glasgow's west end. Close to the University of Glasgow, it's a road with many banks, bars and restaurants. They parked on the road and went into the Santander Bank and asked to see the manager. A man in his thirties, wearing a dark suit approached them a minute later. "Can I help you?"

"Are you the manager?" asked DI McColl.

"Yes. Martin McCann," he said, offering his hand for them to shake.

DI McColl and DS Henderson introduced themselves and asked if there was somewhere confidential to talk. Martin McCann led them to an office at the back of the bank, opened the door and invited them to take a seat.

"Now, what can I do for you?" he asked, eager to help.

DI McColl explained, "We're investigating a series of murders and we believe that one of the victims transferred a large sum of money to this bank in October 2004."

He gave Martin McCann the piece of paper with the account details on it. "We're hoping you can tell us whose account this is, or was."

"Just a minute," said Martin McCann, typing his log in name and password into the desktop computer that sat on the desk. He pressed a few buttons and got to the screen he wanted. He glanced at the piece of paper and keyed in the account number.

"Here we are," he said. "The account was closed down in 2007 but, in 2004, it was in the name of a Roy Campbell, 48 First Avenue, Bearsden. £304,710.20 paid in on the fifteenth of October, 2004. It earned some interest – not much – and then

£305,000 was transferred to an account in Spain in 2006. The remaining amount was withdrawn in cash in 2007 and the account was closed."

"I don't suppose you've got any record of where it was paid to?" asked DI McColl.

Martin McCann pressed some more buttons on the computer and then said, "It was paid to a company called Costa Del Sol Properties in Benalmadena near Malaga."

DI McColl looked at DS Henderson who was noting everything. "So, the Campbells bought a property in Spain with the money."

Martin McCann asked, "Is this what you were looking for?"

"Yes. It tells us that Mr Campbell did have a lot of money back then, and it tells us what he did with it. Can we get a print out of this?"

"Of course," said Martin McCann, pushing a button. The printer at the side of the desk started to make noises and, in a few seconds, two A4 sheets of white paper spewed out onto a tray.

"There you are. There's a note of the account name and there's a print of the transfer to Spain."

McColl and Henderson thanked Martin McCann very much and went back to their car.

"What a crafty old devil," said McColl. "He and his wife pocketed the lot. But the big question is – did anyone else know about it?"

DS Henderson grinned and said, "I think we need to suggest to 'Meek' that we go and check this out. How about a week on the

Costa Del Sol? All expenses paid. All in the interests of being thorough, of course."

"Well, you can try asking him then," replied DI McColl, laughing.

They put on their sunglasses, drove back to the Police Station and told DCI McMeekin what they had just found out.

"So," said DCI McMeekin. "Could this be a motive? Did someone know where the money came from? Did they think they should've got a share of it? Were Mr and Mrs Campbell planning to leave the country? This is getting more and more baffling. Right – leave this just now but start checking the names and addresses of these ex-Scouts."

McColl and Henderson went back to their desks in the main office.

"We'll start going through this against the electoral role and see if these boys or their families still live at these addresses," said DI McColl. "Then we can start going to see them. We can expand the list if they give us some more names and we can find out if any of them know anything. And we can eliminate any of them who were away on the dates of the accidents."

For the next three days, DI McColl and DS Henderson worked their way through the lists. They had the names of over thirty ex-members and had managed to find the addresses for all but two of them. They'd gone to all the houses and spoken with the young men or their families and had managed to establish that nine of them had been able to prove that they were out of the country on holiday, one lived overseas, one worked on an oil rig in the North Sea and two were away serving in the Forces. They tried to establish the whereabouts of the others but this was difficult as they didn't know when the accidents had been set up. They also obtained another twelve names and addresses to follow up.

One or two of the young men had said the same as Pete McNeil, that they didn't like Mr Campbell very much. Some of them had only been in the group for a very short time and had then left.

* * * * *

Friday 13th August, 2010

Jack Craig called back. "We put a note in Wednesday's paper just as you asked. Already, five ex-members have replied. I'll come down and hand in the list for you, and we'll print it again in this week's edition."

An e-mail arrived for DI McColl with a four page attachment which gave the details of the Scottish Gas investigation. They had arrived at the house the night it blew up and their safety engineers had already made the area safe by turning off the gas supply. With the help of the Fire and Rescue officers, they had been able to establish that there had been a leak of gas in the ground floor of the building which, due to the open design of the house, had then spread right through both levels of the house. That much gas would easily cause an explosion of that size and, with gas throughout, the house had been instantly destroyed.

DI McColl asked DS Henderson, "What state is the house in now? I mean, has anyone gone over it once the bodies were recovered?"

DS Henderson replied, "I don't know. It's not been a Police matter until now. I presume it's just a heap of rubble, fenced off probably, and the insurance people might be checking it."

"Have you got the address there? Let's go and have a look."

McColl and Henderson drove to the remains of number 48 First Avenue. The pile of rubble, wood, plaster and broken glass sat behind a wire fence. There was a 'Do Not Enter' sign on the front.

McColl got out his mobile phone and rang DCI McMeekin. He told him where they were and asked if he could get a Fire and Rescue investigator to come and meet them there.

While they waited for him to arrive, they spoke to the Campbell's neighbours. They told them all about the night when they'd been woken up by the explosion, how they came out to find the house destroyed and bits of debris all over the road and gardens. Their car had been in their driveway and it had a large chunk of wall on its roof and through the windscreen, and they told them that the Campbells had indeed bought a villa in Spain a few years ago.

"They'd gone there on holiday a couple of times and fell in love with the area so they'd bought a place of their own. It was newly built and had its own garden and pool. Perhaps they planned to retire over there."

McColl and Henderson also established that the Campbells usually went to bed about 11:30pm and the explosion had happened about 4:00am so the gas must have built up for over four hours.

Andrew Robertson, the Investigator from Strathclyde Fire Brigade arrived and introduced himself. "Hi. Andrew Robertson. Andy. What are you looking for?" he asked them.

"Well, the place is obviously a total mess, but we need to find out if there was a genuine gas leak or had someone left something turned on," explained DI McColl. "Or, could someone have deliberately turned on all the gas?"

"Do you think that's what happened?" said Andy. "Is that why it's a Police matter?"

"Well, we have our suspicions," answered DI McColl.

"We didn't really investigate the cause. We left that to the Scottish Gas experts," said Andy.

"Can we go in to have a look around?" asked DI McColl. "Is it safe?"

"You'll need protective footwear, gloves and hard hats before you go in there. I've got a load of them in my car. I'll find something that should fit you."

Once McColl and Henderson were suitably kitted out with safety gear, Andy Robertson pulled part of the wire fence back and the three of them went in. They spent an hour carefully moving some of the smaller bits of debris and they found some things that were recognisable. Then DS Henderson exclaimed, "Hey! This is what we want!"

The other two looked over. DS Henderson was picking up the mangled metallic hob from the Campbell's cooker. "Look at this," he said.

Despite the explosion and the damage caused by all the rubble, it was still possible to see the hob and the four knobs which were used to turn on the gas rings. They were all turned on to their full setting.

"So, that's where the gas came from," said DI McColl.

"It certainly looks like it," agreed Andy.

"Right. Let's take this away," said DI McColl. "And we can go and see the Scottish Gas investigators with it."

They thanked Andy Robertson for his time and his help as they changed out of their safety gear and back into their normal shoes.

DS Henderson's trousers were covered in dust. "I don't suppose you've got a brush in there?" he said to Andy.

"I do," he replied. "Don't worry. It's not the first time this has happened."

He handed DS Henderson a clothes brush from the boot of his car and Henderson got tidied up as much as he could. He gave the brush back to Andy. They thanked him again and went back to their car.

McColl and Henderson got the address for the Scottish Gas investigators and drove to their office. They got out of their car, went to the reception and introduced themselves. Within a minute, a man appeared and said he was one of the investigators at the Campbell's house. His identity badge gave his name as Alan Cameron.

He took them through to his office. Henderson was carrying the metal hob which he gave to Alan Cameron.

"We found this in the rubble at 48 First Avenue," said DI McColl. "It's mangled but it appears that all four hobs were turned fully on. We're assuming that that couldn't have happened in the blast."

Alan Cameron nodded. "No, that's impossible. So all four were on full? I take it you don't think the couple left them on accidentally."

"No, said DI McColl. "We suspect that someone else deliberately turned them on. We don't know how yet, but we think someone got into the house, turned these on and then scarpered before the place went up."

He continued, "If these were all on full, how long would it take for the house to fill with gas and blow up?"

"It depends a lot on where the flame or spark came from that set it off," said Alan Cameron. "Four on full would let a lot of gas into the house, and quickly. It would take less than thirty minutes for the place to go up."

"So, if the couple went to bed at 11:30, these couldn't have been left on then as the house would have blown up around midnight, instead of four o'clock."

"That's what it looks like," agreed Alan Cameron. "Someone's turned these on thirty minutes or so before the explosion – which would give him time to be miles away." He thought for a moment. "What kind of night was it?" he asked.

"It was during those two weeks of hot weather," said DS Henderson. "Why?"

Alan Cameron explained, "If it was hot muggy weather, which actually, I do seem to remember it was at the time, it's likely that they've had a window open during the night. Some of the gas would escape out the open window and that might have slowed down the time it took to explode."

"But, if a ground floor window was accidentally left open," said DI McColl. "That could have let our mystery attacker into the house. He could have turned on the gas, then climbed back out the window, and probably pushed it closed behind him to stop the gas getting out, and then he's got out of there as fast as he could."

"But", said Alan Cameron. "Why not just kill the two of them in their bed? Why blow up the whole house?"

"That's easy," said McColl. "To make it look like an accident. That's what you guys and the fire investigators both thought. He's been miles away – he might have had a car or a bike a few streets away, and he's got away as fast as he could. The house explodes

99

and everyone thinks it was a gas leak. Simple. He could even have waited somewhere until he heard the explosion, just to make sure."

"Could he have left something in the house, timed to spark to set off the explosion?" asked DS Henderson.

"That's possible as well," said Alan Cameron. "It'd never be found under all that rubble and mess. And he would never expect this hob to be found under all the debris either."

"Well, we don't know for sure how it's been set off," said McColl. "But, we do know that someone had turned on the gas deliberately. So, we can escalate this up to a murder enquiry."

McColl and Henderson thanked Alan Cameron for his time and his help and they said goodbye.

"Any time," said Alan Cameron. "Happy to have been a help."

They went back to their car and phoned DCI McMeekin. They told him all they'd found.

"The forensic guys are still going through all the food containers from Paul Thompson's house. They got a lot of stuff out of the bins. And, we've also got hold of the lawnmower from Stephen Moffat's. I'm getting someone to have a good look at that, as well. Right you two, get back in here and we'll go over everything we've got so far."

"Ok," said DI McColl. "We'll be there in about twenty minutes."

DI McColl and DS Henderson got back to Milngavie Police Station and went straight to DCI McMeekin's office.

"You timed that well," said McMeekin. "I've just had a call about the lawnmower. The wiring was badly damaged in places but they're sure that it was tampered with. Someone's done something to the wires in the plug and at the handle. When Stephen Moffat switched it on, the current's gone right through him, killing him instantly."

"So," said DI McColl. "Three of the deaths were caused deliberately. And, if we get anything from forensics about Paul Thompson's food, that could be another one. What do we think about the tent fire? Is that looking more deliberate now, as well?"

"It must be," said McMeekin. "I've got hold of the photos from the local Drymen Police who arrived at the scene. The fire was devastating. It would have taken a lot of petrol or paraffin to cause that much damage so quickly. A lot more than he could possibly have been carrying with him on his walk. So, we have to assume, at this stage, that someone's gone to his tent in the middle of the night, poured fuel all over it, and then set it alight. As John Lindsay's tried to get out, the attacker must have poured on even more fuel and the poor guy's been roasted alive."

"Speak to Mrs Moffat again," said McMeekin. "Find out where they stored their lawnmower and if it was under lock and key. Were there any signs of a break-in?"

DI McColl and DS Henderson went back to the Moffat's house and rang the bell. Christine Moffat answered the door and immediately recognized the two detectives.

"We're sorry to bother you again," said DI McColl. "But we have another question. Can you show us where you kept your lawnmower?"

"I don't understand," said Christine. "Why do you want to see that?"

"Well," said DI McColl. "We have reason to believe someone deliberately tampered with the wiring so that, when your husband's turned it on, he's been electrocuted. We know it wasn't an accident."

"What?" gasped Christine Moffat. She looked as if she was going to faint. DS Henderson was first to react and he held out a hand to support her.

"Are you alright, Mrs Moffat," he said.

"I'll be ok," she replied, catching her breath but starting to cry. "I don't understand. Why would anyone want to harm Stephen? Who could it be?"

"We don't know at the moment," said DI McColl. "Our investigations are still at an early stage. We're just getting various forensic test results."

"And, what about the Campbells?" asked Christine. "Do you think that was deliberate as well?"

"It appears so," said DI McColl

"But, why? It doesn't make any sense."

"That's what we need to find out," said DI McColl. "Now about this lawnmower …"

Christine took them to the garden at the back of the house and showed them the shed. It wasn't locked.

"Do you normally leave it unlocked?" asked DI McColl. "Even when you go away?"

"Yes, we do," said Christine. "I mean, we did. There's nothing here of any real value." Then the grim reality struck her. "Oh God! Someone's got into the shed and done something to the lawnmower when we've been away on holiday! But who? Why?"

"We don't know who or why at this stage. We just needed to find out if it was actually possible for someone to have got into the shed and tampered with the wiring. That's what we suspected must have happened," said DI McColl.

"So, if we'd locked the shed, Stephen would still be alive?"

"I'm afraid we can't say that," said DI McColl. "The person or persons might have found a way in even if it was locked. He, or they, might be clever enough to get into the shed another way. Since we don't yet know who they are, we don't know what they're capable of."

"Now, we asked you before about a large sum of money," said DI McColl, changing the subject.

"Yes, I remember," said Christine.

"We've found out that Roy Campbell sold the Scout Hall and all the equipment and raised over three hundred thousand pounds. He put the money in an account of his own, kept it there a couple of years and then used it to buy a villa in Spain. Did you know anything about this?"

"No. Not a thing," replied Christine. "So, he took the whole lot? For himself?"

"Yes," said DI McColl. "Every penny."

"I suppose I'm not all that surprised," she said. "I met Roy Campbell when Stephen and I got engaged and the group was coming to an end about then. There was always something about him. Something suspicious. Or creepy, you know? That might explain why. But, what could that have to do with Stephen?"

"That's what we're trying to work out," answered DI McColl. "We don't know if that was a motive and we don't know who knew about it. And we don't know if that mystery person thought that all the leaders were involved."

"Well Stephen certainly wasn't," said Christine. "I'd have known if he had a large sum of money like that. He had a good job in IT and got paid well for it. But we were never involved in anything like that."

"Yes," said DI McColl. "The Campbells took all the money. We know that. But, did that get them killed?"

They were just about to leave when McColl's phone started ringing. It was DCI McMeekin.

"Yes, Chief?" said McColl.

"We've just had a call from the Security Officer at Morrison's supermarket, Gary Woods" said DCI McMeekin. "He's found something interesting on their CCTV. You'd better get down there and see it."

"On our way," replied McColl.

He and Henderson left Christine Moffat, promising to keep her advised of any developments, and drove to Anniesland, to the Morrison's car park. On the way, DI McColl explained to DS Henderson what DCI McMeekin had told him.

They arrived, parked their car, went in and asked for Gary Woods. The girl at the Customer Service Desk called him and he came down from his office. McColl and Henderson introduced themselves and asked what he had found.

He took them to his office where there were several CCTV monitors showing the store entrance and many of the aisles. Shoppers filled their baskets and trolleys mostly unaware that they were being constantly watched. Gary Woods' job was to watch for shoplifters in the store or anyone tampering with the products.

"Have a look at this screen here," he said pointing to a large monitor. He clicked a button and the screen came on. It was a black and white picture of an aisle in the store. "This is a recording from Tuesday the third of August. You can see the date and time in the corner of the screen. Mr Smith asked me to have a look through my recordings to see if there was anything suspicious going on."

The recording was rather jerky but a man carrying a shopping basket appeared. DS Henderson recognized him right away. "That's Paul Thompson." he said.

"That's right," said Gary Woods. "Just watch what happens."

They watched Paul Thompson pick up a tin of something and put it in his basket. Then he looked at a shelf and put his basket on the floor. He then appeared to try to get something down from the top shelf which he couldn't reach. He stood up and stretched to get it as another person appeared on the screen. A thin looking man wearing a plain dark top with the hood pulled over his head.

"Watch what he does," said Gary Woods.

The man appeared to kneel down beside Paul Thompson's shopping basket. He had something in his hand but they couldn't make out what it was. A pen? He pushed whatever it was inside Paul Thompson's basket and stood up again. It took less than two seconds. Then he disappeared from view as Paul Thompson stepped back from the shelf with a tin in his hand which he put in the basket as he picked it up.

Gary Woods clicked another button and the screen changed to show what looked like the same man, with his hood still up, walking out of the store.

"He's not made a purchase, or used a card, I'm afraid, or you could have identified him that way," said Gary Woods. "He's just waited for his opportunity, done whatever he did, and then got out of the store as fast as he could."

"Don't tell us you've got him going back to a car next?" asked DI McColl expectantly. "With a clear view of the registration number?"

"Afraid not," replied Gary Woods. "The CCTV concentrates on the outer door area. There are some cameras in the car-park but we've not picked him up on any of them."

"Can we see it again?" asked DI McColl.

Gary Woods played the recording again. What was in the man's hand?

"Could it be a syringe?" asked DS Henderson. "Can you zoom in on it?"

Gary Woods pushed a button and the image froze on the screen. He pushed another and it zoomed in on the man's hand. It wasn't particularly clear but they were sure it was a syringe. The man appeared to be injecting something into Paul Thompson's shopping.

"This is really helpful," said DI McColl. He turned to DS Henderson. "Do we know who this guy is?"

DS Henderson shook his head. "No idea," he said. "We'll need to try and get a clear image of him from the recording first."

"Do we know what Paul Thompson had in his basket?" asked DI McColl.

"Yes. We do," said Gary Woods. "He paid at the till with his staff card and I've got a print out of his receipt. Here." He handed it to McColl.

"Coffee, milk, custard creams," read McColl aloud. "Two tins of soup, a tin of custard and some bananas." He looked at DS Henderson. "The bananas! Of course! This guy could have injected a large enough dose of the poison into one or more of the bananas. He's eaten the poisoned one the evening he died."

He turned to Gary Woods. "Can I take this receipt? And can we get a copy of this CCTV recording?"

"Of course," said Gary Woods "I've put the recording on this disc for you." He handed DI McColl a computer disc. "This should work on your computers. If you need any more stuff, let me know." Woods was thrilled at being part of an important investigation instead of his usual routine of sitting watching dozens of screens. This made him feel very important and he would be able to boast to his friends that the Police had come to ask him for help with a major investigation.

They thanked him and made their way out of the store. McColl called DCI McMeekin and told him the good news.

"Bring it back here," he said. "And we'll see if we can get a good image from it. Are you sure he's not one of the Scouts you've already spoken to?"

"No," said McColl. "Neither of us recognise him. We're sure he's not on our list so far."

"Ok. We'll get some copies and you can start showing it to all the Scout ex-members on your list. Meanwhile, I'll tell the forensic guys to concentrate on any banana skins they've recovered from Paul Thompson's bins."

DI McColl and DS Henderson returned to the Police Station with the copy of the CCTV recording and put the disc into one of their desktop computers. They played the recording for DCI McMeekin's benefit. "The picture's not really that clear, is it?" he commented. "You can only see part of the guy's face. We get a general impression of his height and build but that's about it. Give the disc to one of the computer boffins and see if they can make it any clearer, and if we can get a usable print of his face."

The Police had a computer expert, or geek, who was used to investigating confiscated computers to see what was stored or hidden on them that could be used as evidence. They gave him the disc and asked him to see what he could do to improve the image and get a print from it.

"Leave it with me," he said.

"Needless to say, it's top priority, so if you could ..." said DI McColl.

"Isn't it always," he replied. "I'll be as quick as I can."

Ten

DCI McMeekin was sitting in his office when there was a knock on the open door. He looked up. One of the forensic team walked in carrying a sheet of paper.

"We went through all the stuff in Paul Thompson's kitchen and bins liked you asked. And you were right", he said. "We found two banana skins in his bin. They were black but the chemical analysis of one is exactly what we'd expect to find but the other has traces of a toxin all over it. It does appear to have had a substantial amount of aconitine added to it. There was a large concentration on one bit of the skin and we found a tiny puncture there suggesting it had been injected. It's all in here". He handed the paper to McMeekin.

"That's just what we wanted," said DCI McMeekin. "We've got a CCTV recording showing an unknown man apparently injecting something into the victim's shopping and we suspected it was this poison. We don't know where the guy's got it from though or why he's targeted the victim but this appears to prove what happened. Thanks for getting this."

DCI McMeekin called McColl and Henderson into his office and told them about the forensic report.

"So, it was this aconitine poison that was used. So, we've definitely got four murders and all planned to look like accidents. At the moment, we're only assuming this guy's an ex-Scout. He might not be. There might be some other reason why he's killed these leaders. And, we don't even know if he's working alone. For all we know, there could be two or three of them working together. Any luck with the photo of the poisoner?"

"We should have it shortly," said McColl. "And then we can go back round the Scouts we've already spoken to and see if any of them can identify him. Are we thinking of releasing it to the media, to widen the search?"

"No. Not yet," said DCI McMeekin. "See if the Scouts come up with anything first. We're thinking that this guy, or these guys maybe, believe they've got away with it so far. If he or they suddenly finds out we're after them, they might disappear. We're supposing that there are no more potential victims that he's after so keep trying with the Scouts.

There was another knock at DCI McMeekin's door and the computer expert came in, holding some photos in his hand.

"These are the best I can get," he said. "I've cleaned the image and lightened it a bit. You can see about two thirds of his face under the hood."

He distributed the photos to the three detectives.

McColl and Henderson could see a big improvement on the picture they'd seen on Morrison's CCTV screen. The man's hair was covered so they couldn't even know what colour it was or if he had shaved it off.

"Right," said DCI McMeekin. "Go round all the Scouts you've spoken to already. See if anyone recognises this guy. You've already said that he doesn't look like anyone you've spoken to. But, if he was working in a group, see if any of them react to the photo. I want this guy's name and details. Someone must know who he is, and at the moment, the only people you can ask are these ex-Scouts. On you go and let me know the moment you get anything."

DCI McMeekin's phone started ringing as McColl and Henderson left his office. They went back to their desks and got the list of all the Scouts names and addresses. Thirty five names to check again, less the few who didn't live in the area any more. They went through the addresses and planned their route. It was late on Friday afternoon and they supposed that the best time to visit these young men to get them at home was in the early evening, and again the next day.

The first few ex-members that they visited didn't recognise the man in the photo. McColl and Henderson asked them again if they could remember any more names. "Who did you usually go with? Who did you stand next to? Who did you always pick for your team? Who sat beside you at summer camp? Who sat beside you in the minibus? Who was in the same tent as you?"

They managed to get a few more names to add to their list but were having no luck with anyone identifying the man in the photo.

Saturday 14th August 2010

On the Saturday afternoon, when they were down to the last few names on the list, they finally got something positive. One of the ex-members thought they recognised the young man but he couldn't remember his name. "Are you certain?" asked DI McColl. The man stared again at the picture.

"There was a guy. He joined for a short time and then left again. He was hardly a member for any length of time so most folk will probably have forgotten him. He was a wee fair haired boy. He joined in the New Year or the spring and attended sporadically. He did go to the summer camp though. He was always homesick or something like that. He was always crying in the tent like he wanted to go home to his mum. He didn't really join in with the activities like everyone else. But I just can't remember his name.

He wasn't from around here, I don't think. We didn't know him from school or anything like that. I couldn't say for definite. It was years ago and I can't really see his face properly."

"Please try and remember his name," said DI McColl. A thought struck him and he asked "Do you have any old photographs perhaps? That you took at the summer camp? Could he be in any of them?"

"No. I never took a camera with me. But, wait a minute. One of the leaders used to wander about with a camera all the time. He took lots of pictures and sometimes some videos as well."

"Which one of them was it?" asked DI McColl.

"Mr Lindsay. John Lindsay."

McColl looked at Henderson. "Are you thinking what I'm thinking?"

"Yes," he replied. "Could these pictures still be somewhere in his house?"

"Exactly! We'd better go and search the place." He turned back to the ex-Scout. "Do you know what year that might have been?"

"I'm not sure. Possibly 2001 or 2002," he replied. "I think it was one of the last camps."

They thanked him and went back to the Police Station. DS Henderson found John Lindsay's address and they applied for a search warrant.

* * * * *

The Scout summer camp was a major event and, every July, they went away for 10 days, usually to somewhere right beside the coast. North Berwick, Arbroath, Mull or Islay were the usual sites and they stayed on farms, not on official camp sites. They had a big tent, a marquee, where they had tables and benches for their meals, a cook tent with gas ovens and a gas fridge, a water boiler, and an area for washing. There were two or three boys' tents, each with an older boy in charge. There was a staff tent and a storage tent and they were arranged around a large square which had a flagpole in the centre. Away from the square, they had toilet tents and a games area. It was all very well organized. Mr Campbell, two of the leaders and some of the older boys took all the stuff in a big van and set it all up on the Saturday. Paul Thompson took the rest of the boys in a hired minibus on the Sunday or Monday. He brought them home at the end of the camp while those who had set it all up, dismantled everything, packed it away and brought it back to Bearsden.

While they were away, they played games in the field or on the beach, went swimming in the sea when the weather was good, went for walks, had inter-tent competitions and, on the last night, they had a bonfire barbecue. John Lindsay usually did all the cooking and there was a tuck shop where boys could also buy drinks, crisps, sweets and chocolates.

It was all planned with military precision and was the highlight of their year. When they got good weather, everyone had a great time. If it was wet, alternative arrangements had to be made and they went to the nearest town to the swimming baths or to the cinema.

When it was announced in January where they'd be going that summer, the boys all started to get excited, looking forward to it. They paid their deposits and could pay up the rest of it in instalments each week. The tents and equipment were brought out of storage in May and any repairs or maintenance was done between then and July. All the food supplies were bought from

Morrison's supermarket in bulk since Paul Thompson got a staff discount there, and everything was packed into large boxes or hampers ready to go into the van.

* * * * *

There was nothing else McColl and Henderson could do so they decided to resume on Sunday morning. They bade each other a goodnight and went their separate ways. John McColl went home to his wife and two boys for his usual Saturday routine – a Chinese take-away dinner, a beer and some TV. His older son, Johnny, had developed a taste for chicken chop-suey and fried rice but their younger boy, Gregor, who was eight was a rather fussy eater and wouldn't even try a taste of the take-away. Lynne McColl had to make him something that he liked instead. McColl phoned home first to let them know that he was on his way and then he phoned the Chinese restaurant to place his usual order so that he could collect it on his way home.

Scott Henderson wasn't married but lived with his partner, Suzy. They would just have a quiet night in – unless she had made any plans that he didn't know about yet. Saturday evening was their chance to wind down from all the pressures of the week. He usually preferred to stay in, watching the television but arrangements were sometimes made without him being consulted.

John McColl and Scott Henderson were good friends as well as being colleagues and, once a month, they spent Saturday evenings with Lynne and Suzy who also got on well. They would eat out at one of their favourite local restaurants or, sometimes, Lynne would cook dinner if the McColls couldn't arrange for someone to look after the boys for the evening. Johnny and Gregor really liked their "aunt" Suzy as she always brought them chocolate or sweets when she came to visit. Unfortunately for the boys, this wasn't one of those arranged evenings and the 'grown-ups' had other plans.

Eleven

The search warrant for John Lindsay's home had been given top priority and had arrived so McColl and Henderson drove to the address and got out of the car.

John Lindsay had lived alone. He was thirty six when he was killed and his parents had been devastated when they were told what had happened to him. It was now several weeks since his death and they were spending the day going through the slow and painful process of clearing out his flat so that it could be sold. They were both at the flat when McColl and Henderson arrived and introduced themselves at the door.

"We're really sorry to bother you at this time," said DI McColl. "But we want to search the premises. We do have a warrant. We're looking for any photographs or video that John took when he was in the 130th Bearsden Scout Group."

"But, what do you want those for?" asked Mrs Lindsay. "And why are the Police even involved?"

"I really hate to tell you this," said DI McColl. "But, we have reason to believe that John's death was not accidental. All four of the Scout leaders died last month and we think it's too much of a coincidence. We are treating these deaths as deliberate and, at this stage, we think it might have been an ex-member of the Scout group."

Mrs Lindsay couldn't believe what she was hearing. She suddenly felt light-headed and had to sit down. Mr Lindsay sat beside her and tried to comfort her.

McColl went on. "Mr and Mrs Roy Campbell were killed when their house was flattened by a gas explosion and we believe someone broke in and turned on the gas deliberately. Stephen Moffat was electrocuted by his lawnmower and we're certain that someone had tampered with it. Paul Thompson was poisoned and we've got CCTV pictures which seem to show someone injecting something into some bananas he bought at his supermarket. As you know, there was a sudden fire in John's tent. Our investigations lead us to believe that it would have taken a lot more paraffin or fuel to start that than John could possibly have been carrying with him."

The Lindsays sat listening, unable to believe what they were hearing.

"The only thing that links these four victims – well, five as there was Mrs Campbell as well - is that they were all leaders in the Scout Group that stopped operating seven years ago. We've since found out that Mr Campbell was involved in some financial wrongdoing with the Scout funds – but we don't know if that was the motive behind these killings. We've been putting together a list of as many ex-members as we can, and we've been going round speaking to them. And one of them told us that John was in the habit of taking lots of photos and videos of their summer camp. We were hoping to get a look at these pictures."

"Do you still have them?" asked DI McColl. "And, do you know where they are?"

"I think so," said Mrs Lindsay. "There are boxes of stuff in a cupboard in John's room. I'll show you." She stood up and led McColl and Henderson through to John's bedroom.

"We've cleared out all his clothes and books. We gave them to a charity shop. But it's been a really slow process. We can hardly bring ourselves to do this." She opened a cupboard door and inside were shelves of boxes.

"We've not gone through this stuff yet. If they're anywhere, they'll be in here somewhere," she said. "You're welcome to look through them."

She left them to it and went to rejoin her husband. McColl and Henderson lifted the boxes out and put them on top of the bed. John Lindsay had meticulously labelled them and they soon found the box containing the photos from The Scouts. There were photos and strips of old negatives for the ones prior to 2001. He'd obviously bought a digital camera that year as all the ones since then were saved on discs.

"We don't know what year our mystery boy was there," said McColl. "We'll need to take the lot and go through them back at the station."

They picked up the box and took it through to Mr and Mrs Lindsay.

"These seem to be what we're looking for," said DI McColl. "We're going to take this box away to look through. We'll take copies of anything we need and we'll return everything to you as soon as we can. I'm really sorry you had to find out this way. We're still not a hundred percent sure that it was murder but it does look like it."

"Will you let us know?" asked Mrs Lindsay, tearfully.

"Of course we will," said DI McColl. "We've got all your contact details, so we can let you know any developments. We can arrange for a Family Liaison Officer to come and speak to you about the investigation. Do you want us to do that?"

Mr and Mrs Lindsay looked at each other, not knowing what to think. Mr Lindsay spoke, "We got a terrible shock a few weeks ago, and now you've come and given us an even bigger shock. We can't really think straight at the moment but what you're suggesting might be a good idea."

McColl and Henderson promised to arrange it and thanked the Lindsays for their time and apologised once more for being the bearers of such tragic news. They took the box out to their car and drove back to the Police Station.

Back at the Police Station, they cleared a space on DI McColl's desk to make room to work.

"Right," said DS Henderson. "What are we looking for? A picture of a boy from seven or more years ago who looks like the guy in the CCTV with half his face hidden?"

"Yes. That's it, in a nutshell."

"In other words, a needle in a haystack? And we're not even sure what the needle looks like."

DCI McMeekin was also working that day. He'd seen them come back in and heard them talking. He came over to DI McColl's desk.

"What've you got there?" he asked them.

They explained that they'd met the Lindsays and had got a box of photos from the Scout Camps and that they were about to start looking through them.

DS Henderson got two black coffees and they began looking through the photos.

"At least he kept a good filing system," said DI McColl. "They're all sorted into years, into summer camp and 'others' so it's quite methodical. Look – 2002: North Berwick, 2001: Arbroath, 2000: Goswick- wherever that is - 1999: Mull, 1998: Stranraer, and so on," he read as he lifted the bundles out of the box. There were about fifty photos for each year's camp.

"Some of them are just views of the area or the campsite. We need to look at any that have got the boys in them."

They started looking carefully through the hundreds of photos, pausing to stare at any which showed the boys' faces. They could already recognise some of them as they'd been the ex-members that they'd already interviewed.

"Look at this," said DS Henderson. "In 2002, there are group shots of the boys from each tent. They're lined up in front with the oldest boy at the end, right down to the youngest. They all seem pretty happy except for this boy here." He pointed to a fair haired boy at the end of the line, obviously the youngest of the group but he was looking down at his feet instead of smiling at the camera like all the others.

"He must be the wee fair haired boy. It could have been his first time away from home. He looks rather homesick, don't you think?"

"See if he's in any of the others," said DI McColl.

DS Henderson went through all the others for 2002. There were photos of the boys on the beach, playing football, building sandcastles, running races or just lying in their tents. Eventually, he found one with the homesick boy in it. He was standing at the side watching the inter-tent races going on and they could now see his face. He was a normal looking boy but he was standing on his own and seemed to be wrapped up in his own thoughts.

The two detectives stared at the picture. DI McColl was first to speak.

"Whoever he is, he doesn't look like any of the ex-members we've spoken to. Does he? Are there any more of him?"

"He appears in a couple of the prints but he's standing in the background, on his own. No wonder he was homesick. None of the other boys seemed to talk to him."

"But look at the shape of his nose and chin. Now compare them to our mystery CCTV man. They're very alike, aren't they?"

"Can we get this enlarged?"

They made arrangements to get ten copies made of an enlarged picture of the boy's face. They wouldn't be ready that night so they decided to call it a day. They would re-start their search the next morning once they had the enlargements.

Twelve

Monday 16th August 2010

This was a big day in the McColl household. John and Lynne's older son was starting senior school that day. He came down for breakfast wearing his new school uniform and, to both his parents, he suddenly looked much older than he had the night before.

John McColl wished him good luck. "You'll get on fine. You'll make lots of new friends. Just pay attention to everything you get told. I'll hear all about it later."

He got up and put on his jacket, said cheerio to the boys, kissed Lynne goodbye and headed outside to his car. He turned on the car radio as he drove the short distance to Milngavie Police Station but he wasn't really listening to what they were saying. His mind was already drifting ahead to what he might find out that day.

When DI McColl arrived at the police station, there was an A4 envelope already sitting on his desk, marked with his name. There were ten copies of the enlargement as requested. DS Henderson arrived a minute later and, after asking each other how their evening had been, they both sat staring at the face of the boy.

"He must be the homesick boy we heard about, said DI McColl." The more I look at him, the more I'm convinced he's the man at the supermarket. But, perhaps I just want him to look like that. Let's go and see some of the ex-members we've spoken to and see if we can put a name to this boy."

DS Henderson's desk phone rang and he reached over and picked it up.

"Hi. It's Jack Craig here, from The Milngavie and Bearsden Herald."

"Oh. Hi. How are you?" replied DS Henderson.

"Fine thanks," replied Jack Craig. "I've not had that much more success with ex-members' names. I've just got one more."

He read out the name and address to DS Henderson who recognised it immediately as one they already had.

"Have you got anything new?" asked Jack Craig. "Anything that I can print in this week's edition? I've been sitting tight on this story for weeks and we want to print it before any of the 'big boys' get hold of it."

"Not yet," replied DS Henderson, glancing at DI McColl and scribbling Craig's name to let him know who he was speaking to. "Don't worry. None of the media have got anything about this. I can't tell you much more at the moment except that our investigations are ongoing."

"That's not much, is it?"

"All I can tell you at the moment is that we've been speaking to lots of ex-Scouts, the families of the victims and Paul Thompson's colleagues at Morrison's. We think we've got a potential motive but that's not definite yet. We also got a lead on a load of photographs that John Lindsay took at the Scout summer camps and we're going through them – but that's about it so far. We're just about to go and speak to a few ex-members just now. I'll call you in the next couple of days if we find out anything. Is that ok?"

"I guess so. Good luck. Just remember who it was that told you about this," said Jack Craig.

They ended the conversation and DS Henderson told DI McColl what they'd been saying.

DI McColl drank the last of his coffee, which was getting cold, and stood up. "Come on let's go. Who are we going to see first?"

Before they could even move from their desks, DCI McMeekin came walking towards them from his office. "Morning, you two. I see you've got the photo enlargments."

They both nodded, and said a 'good morning' to their superior.

"I've been thinking," said DCI McMeekin. "What if the money's not the motive? We're just supposing that it is since we don't have anything else to go on. Campbell took the money and spent it – but that was years ago. Why wait until now? Could there be something else? The only people who might have been angry at not getting a share of the money are all dead too. Nobody else seems to have been involved with the money – maybe that's not it. We're assuming it's the Scouts but it might not be the money. What else could it be? And why wait seven years to do anything? Is there something recent? Could someone have been blackmailing one or more of them?"

"But we're fumbling about in the dark," said DI McColl. "What do you want us to try next?"

"I think we're going to have to search the houses with a fine toothed comb. Look at all their papers, their mail, check their computers, their bank accounts. Look for anything unusual. Check their phone records. Were there any calls that were suspicious? Speak to all their work colleagues. Were any of them behaving suspiciously? Was there any trouble at their places of work? Were their families aware of anything? Anything at all?"

"We're going to need some extra man power on this," said DI McColl, glancing at DS Henderson for support. "We can't do all of this ourselves."

"Alright," said DCI McMeekin. "I'll draft in some uniformed officers to do some of the house searches and to speak to their work colleagues. You two can get their computers checked and can go through everything that comes back from these questions."

DCI McMeekin got three uniformed officers drafted in to help with the searches and interviews. Milngavie was not the biggest police station and it was not unknown for an officer to be dealing with a member of the public at the front desk and yet have to be interrupted to go and deal with a serious road traffic incident. 'Meek' explained to the officers exactly what was required. DI McColl and DS Henderson already knew that John Lindsay's house had already been half emptied by his parents so they might not find anything useful if it even existed.

Christine Moffat was reluctant to let the officers take away Stephen's laptop and was even less enthusiastic when they asked to go through all Stephen's papers and bank details. She phoned her father to ask for his advice and he more or less told her that she had to let them go ahead. *Anything that might help them solve this.* There was nothing unusual or suspicious in any of his papers so they took the laptop back to the detectives. Christine had explained that Stephen actually worked in an IT job and always had the latest models so he'd only had that laptop for six months or so. His old one was up in their loft and she got it down for them.

The police station's resident geek looked through all the folders on the laptops but found nothing of any use to them so they could be returned to Christine the next day.

When the officers went to John Lindsay's house, there was no sign of the computer that DI McColl and DS Henderson remembered seeing when they visited. Mr and Mrs Lindsay said that they had taken it back to their own house so it was quickly retrieved.

"I don't really know how to use it," said Mr Lindsay. "I mean I hardly know how to switch it on but I thought I might try to learn."

The geek got to work on it and discovered that there were some folders with odd names that were encrypted. It didn't take him long to get them opened and, as soon as he saw what they contained, he called the two detectives over to see what he'd found.
The encrypted folders contained a lot of pictures, which appeared to have been from the Scout summer camps but, unlike the other ones showing the boys at their activities, these seemed to show the boys getting changed for swimming or to play on the beach.

DI McColl and DS Henderson stared at the pictures on the screen and then looked at each other.

DS Henderson spoke first. "Now, we didn't expect to see anything like that, did we?"

None of the pictures were close-ups and, depending on how they were looked at, they were either some shots that might have been taken at random showing the boys getting changed – or there was something darkly suspicious about them. It could be argued either way.

The geek spoke, "Why would he have these in an encrypted folder with an odd name? If these were extra shots not to be included in the ones of the camp, why not delete them? What was he up to?"

"I don't know," said DI McColl. "But, see if there are any more like them."

In total, there were three folders of similar pictures. None of them showed anything indecent or illegal but it was a mystery as to why they were there in the first place.

According to the geek, John Lindsay had viewed these pictures on a number of occasions, at fairly regular intervals.

When McColl and Henderson told DCI McMeekin about this new development, he told them to get hold of John Lindsay's collection of videos. Not just the ones he shot at the camps but any other videos or DVDs that were in his house.

Mr and Mrs Lindsay helpfully gave them his digital video camera and all of his tapes and DVDs that they hadn't given to the local charity shop. McColl and Henderson took them back to the police station and started going through them. There were videos of each summer's camp, with titles and credits added and a musical accompaniment. These were all 'above board' and there was nothing untoward on any of them. Until they found a personal DVD recording, dated 2002, which was entitled "Private – Camp extras". McColl and Henderson put it into their player and began to watch.

"What the …?"

What they saw horrified them. They paused it and quickly called 'Meek' from his office to come and see it with them. McColl put it back to the beginning and pressed the play button. The recording clearly showed Roy Campbell, Paul Thompson and Stephen Moffat – obviously John Lindsay was doing the recording. It was semi-dark but it was obviously inside a tent. The three men had hold of a boy – the fair haired, homesick loner they recognised from the photographs. They held him tightly down on top of a sleeping bag on a camp bed. The boy was struggling in vain. Stephen Moffat had his hand over the boy's mouth so he couldn't scream out. Paul Thompson appeared to have a roll of strong tape

126

and with it he taped the boy's mouth and then they stuck his feet to the bottom of the bed. Stephen Moffat was holding his arms tightly.

What they saw next shocked them to the core. Roy Campbell kneeled down beside the bed and pulled down the boy's pyjama trousers and began touching him all over. After five minutes Paul Thompson took over, and then John Lindsay. The recording eventually stopped and the screen went blank.

The three detectives sat in complete silence, stunned and unable to speak. DI McCall couldn't stop thinking about his own two boys who were about the same age as the boy in the video. He felt absolutely sick.

DCI McMeekin was the first to say something. "I'm sickened. I don't know what to say. That poor boy. It's despicable. Utterly despicable. This shed a new light on the whole thing."

"No wonder he looked homesick and alone in those photos. No wonder he wanted his mum. The poor kid must have been terrified," said DI McColl. "These guys could have got twenty years each if it had come out!"

"My God! Can you imagine if Mr and Mrs Lindsay had sat down to watch that?" said DS Henderson. "The shock would have killed them both."

It all started to fall into place. If the leaders had abused this boy, had he then been the one who'd killed them all? Has he waited seven years and then murdered every one of them?

DCI McMeekin fought to control his emotions and said, "We need to find that boy, that young man. We need to establish if this was an isolated incident or did it happen every summer. No wonder the boys stopped going to the group and it packed in. There could, potentially, be loads of victims of this abuse. They've just not said anything to you when you've spoken to them. Are there other recordings hidden somewhere? In the other leaders' homes? Were they circulated? Were these posted on the internet for other paedophiles to watch? Were these four guys part of a wider organised group? Was the Scout group just a front for their evil activities? Is this why they broke away from the official Scout movement?"

"One or two of the ex-members we spoke to said that there was something odd about Roy Campbell. This must be it," said DS Henderson. "Do we now need to go and ask all the other ex-members if they knew this was going on - or if they were victims as well?"

"We need to find out what the scale of this was – and we need to find this boy," said DCI McMeekin. "There are specialist trained officers who look at this sort of thing. You two don't need to see any more and you know that there is counselling available if you need it."

He continued, "We need to be very careful what we do here. We need to be one hundred percent sure of our facts before we go public with this. It's absolutely essential that we find this boy!"

By "we" he obviously meant McColl and Henderson. They had to go back to the ex-members again and show them the old photographs in the hope that this boy could be identified – and then they had to find him.

DCI McMeekin addressed his detectives, "The Force has specialists who deal with this sort of stuff. They get specially trained to look at these kinds of images when there are cases involving this kind of thing. You two don't have to look at it. I'm sorry you had to see that but we obviously didn't know. Mark the DVD and don't let anyone else see it until I call for assistance. Try to put the detail out of your minds. Try not to let it affect your job. You have to find that boy. Let others deal with the DVD."

"What on earth do we say to the ex-members? Do we ask them if they knew or suspected that the leaders were all paedophiles? Was this widespread? Were there even more men involved as well?"

"You'll have to be very discreet," said DCI McMeekin. "Don't go saying anything about the DVD. Just ask if they suspected anything or knew anything?"

As they were about to check their list of ex-members to go and speak to again, DCI McMeekin spoke again, "If you have any concerns with this, if you feel you need to speak to a counselor – don't feel that you can't ask. I don't expect the two of you to have to watch stuff like that. My door, as you know, is always open for the two of you. Speak to me if you need to."

They nodded and let McMeekin go back into his office.

"This case is just getting worse by the day," said DI McColl.

"Who would have thought?" said DS Henderson. "I guess this gave him a strong enough motive to kill them all. You can't really blame him, I guess."
"He should have reported it at the time. He should have told somebody," said DI McColl. "That doesn't give him an excuse to go killing people, does it? And what about poor Mrs Campbell? She got killed as well, remember? And she couldn't have been directly involved."

"Would anyone have believed him?" asked DS Henderson. "We don't know but it could just have been his word against four adults. Unless they saw that recording, of course."

They agreed to go home and get some dinner. McColl would then go to Henderson's so they could go and speak to his neighbour.

When he got home, John McColl got out of his car and went in his front door. Johnny had already changed out of his school uniform in case he spilled any of his dinner on it. *We can't have you messing it up on your first day!* Once John had said hello to everyone, he asked Johnny how his first day had gone. His son showed him all the new books he'd been given and said he got on alright. "We really just got to meet all our teachers and they met us, and we got shown where everything is. We didn't do any real work, and I've got no homework. Great!"

As arranged, that evening, McColl and Henderson went to visit Scott's neighbour, Pete McNeil. His son, Alan, was upstairs and Pete called him to come down. They introduced themselves and then showed him the photographs. He stared at them for a moment, trying to remember all the names.

He started pointing at the boys in the group picture. "There's me. That's 'Weed', 'Winnie', 'Mac', 'Jingles' and 'Donaldo'. God, he looked miserable. Always crying. Always wanting his mum. He was a right wee misery, I don't know why he ever came to the camp."

DI McColl and DS Henderson were delighted that Alan McNeil knew all the boys in the picture.

"This is fantastic," said McColl. "But, we'll need a proper name for this 'Donaldo'."

"Oh, yeah. Of course," said Alan McNeil. "Wilson, Donald Wilson. Known as 'Donaldo' after the footballer, the one who was always falling over looking for free kicks, and crying to the referee when he didn't get his own way. One of the older boys called him that, and it stuck."

At last, McColl and Henderson had a name for their mystery killer. Donald Wilson.

"What was he really like, this boy?" asked DI McColl.

"It's years ago now," said Alan McNeil. "I think his parents were separated and he lived with his mum. She probably sent him to the camp so she wouldn't have to look after him that week during the school holidays. Lots of parents did that. He was quite young. Maybe she thought it would be the making of him. It wasn't. He was so homesick all the time. A lot of the first time campers were like that but, after a few days, they forgot about home and joined in with all the activities. He didn't. He just stood at the side, moping. Some mornings, we would wake up in the tent and hear him crying in his sleeping bag. By the look of him, he'd been crying all night. Poor kid."

It all fell into place. The leaders had been taking Donald Wilson to their tent, perhaps even offering him the chance to phone his mother, and then they'd been subjecting him to the most awful abuse. He would have cried and cried, and the other boys just assumed he was homesick. He couldn't have told them what had really happened.

"Can you remember if there were any other boys as homesick as him?" asked DI McColl.

"Never like that," replied Alan McNeil. "He was the worst I can remember. He never stopped feeling miserable. The whole week. Non-stop."

"Do you know where this boy lived, or still lives?" asked DI McColl. "Do you know where we could find him?"

"I'm not sure," said Alan McNeil. "He didn't live around here. He wasn't at our school. Perhaps his parents used to live here and his mum might have known some other mothers here so she sent 'Harold', sorry Donald, to our Scout group. But I don't know where he lived."

"Ok. We'll try and look him up," said DI McColl, getting up to go. "We'll be in touch if we need to ask you anything more."

Pete McNeil showed McColl and Henderson to the door, full of pride that his son had been the one to 'crack the case'. If this got into the papers, he could tell everyone that Alan had been the 'star witness'.

McColl and Henderson sat in their car. "Real progress at last," said McColl. "We now know who our mystery man is. Now, all we have to do is find him."

Thirteen

The next morning, McColl and Henderson were in early and they told DCI McMeekin all about their progress the night before. Henderson had done a check for any Donald Wilsons within thirty minutes of the old scout hall. There were three listed so they planned their route and set off to find the first one.

They arrived at the first address on their list. It was a fairly large bungalow. They rang the doorbell and an elderly man answered the door.

He was almost seventy years old and said that his name was, indeed, Donald Wilson. He had no connection with the scouts and had no relatives with the same name.

The second house was empty. McColl and Henderson went to the next door neighbour's instead. A woman there opened the door and confirmed that she knew Mr Wilson next door. He'd be at work at that time. The detectives showed her the photograph but she said that didn't look anything like Mr Wilson. He was about forty years old, had reddish hair, was married and had two children at the local school. McColl and Henderson thanked her for her time and went back to their car. Two down and one to go.

The third address was a large detached house with a double garage and a big driveway. The garden was immaculately kept. A lady who identified herself as Mrs Wilson answered the door. She looked to be in her late forties, with plenty of money. They showed her the photographs of the group at the camp and the man in the supermarket. They were definitely not her husband or anyone else in her family. She seemed quite indignant, aghast at the very

133

suggestion. She explained that she did not know any other Donald Wilsons.

Sitting in their car, McColl and Henderson decided that they would need to widen their search. They didn't even know if their Donald Wilson still lived in the area. Perhaps he had travelled some distance to carry out his grisly acts of revenge.

A wider search showed another Donald Wilson living in the town of Kirkintilloch, about ten miles away and one in Clydebank, about five miles away from Bearsden. Both were visited but neither was the man they were after.

Further checks revealed four more families called Wilson, but not Donald, in the region. They were all interviewed but none of them were, or knew, the man they were looking for.

Back at the Police Station, the two detectives sat in DCI McMeekin's office explaining their lack of success.

"So, it appears that he doesn't live anywhere near here or he's changed his name," said DI McColl.

DCI McMeekin rubbed his spectacles with his handkerchief, contemplating what to do next.

"Right. You need to look for every Wilson within a hundred miles. If he's ex-directory or his home is in another name, or he lives with someone else, you need to find him. I think it's time to get his picture released to the media so see if someone knows who or where he is. I'm always reluctant, as you know, to release pictures as there's always a danger that they'll prejudice a jury when we arrest someone and they appear in court, but we're desperate for information so we'll just have to, and hope for the best."

McColl and Henderson agreed. DS Henderson called Jack Craig at The Bearsden and Milngavie Herald since they had promised him an exclusive story. "If we give you a couple of photographs and a name, can you print this and ask the public to contact us immediately if they know him?" asked DS Henderson.

Jack Craig was excited by this new development. "This is Tuesday afternoon and this week's edition is being planned out. We'll have to re-do our front page." He thought for a moment. "Obviously, I want to help and to get the exclusive. We can post the story on our website, too, so some people can see it there. I'll speak to my boss and we can re-do the front page and get this out on tomorrow's front page as I said." He asked them to send him electronic copies of the two photographs, which they quickly did.

Wednesday 18th August 2010

Jack Craig did as he had said and, the next day, The Milngavie and Bearsden Herald's front page had the photos of the young Donald Wilson at the summer camp and the picture taken from Morrison's CCTV footage of the hooded Donald Wilson walking out of their store after he'd injected the poison into Paul Thompson's shopping. There was an appeal for any information asking members of the public to contact the Police either at Milngavie or through the 'Crimestoppers' confidential phone line. It wasn't specific but it said that the Police wanted to interview as soon as possible in connection with a number of suspicious deaths in the Bearsden area.

Thursday 19th August 2010

The following day, the national newspapers and the two Scottish television news programmes had a major Scottish Criminal Justice story to cover, but not one involving murders in Bearsden. The

Scottish Government, in its infinite wisdom, had announced that Abdelbaset al-Megrahi, the man convicted of planting the bomb that blew up Pan Am Flight 103 over the Scottish town of Lockerbie just before Christmas in 1988, was to be released on compassionate grounds. The decision had provoked the United States Secretary of State, Hillary Clinton, to state that the United States categorically disagreed with the decision.

Instead of the appeal being on their front pages as the Police wanted, all the Scottish newspapers displayed the photographs and asked the public for information, inside their editions, saying in more detail that the man was being sought by the Police regarding the killing of five people in Bearsden in July. The detectives waited impatiently for any news and they jumped with anticipation every time their phone rang. The local appeal hadn't prompted any calls but, once it was put out nationally, the public started to make contact.

The electrical store where Donald Wilson worked made contact and told the detectives his full address and said that he hadn't turned up for work that morning. Wednesday was his usual day off but he was due at work on Thursday. They hadn't seen him since the store closed on the Tuesday evening. The manager had tried phoning him but got no reply.

Two of his neighbours also contacted the Police and confirmed Wilson's address. It was in a quiet part of Hardgate, an area between Bearsden and Clydebank close to the A82 dual carriageway that ran from Glasgow, past Dumbarton and north all the way to Inverness. They said he had lived on his own since his mother had died a few years ago. He always kept to himself and didn't really speak to the neighbours and they just thought of him as a loner. He didn't have a telephone so there was no entry for Wilson at that address. They told the Police that his car was still parked outside his house.

DI McColl and DS Henderson got an arrest warrant arranged as quickly as possible and they then went, with two uniformed officers, to Wilson's address. There was no reply when they rang the doorbell. The door was bashed in but the house was empty. There was no sign of Wilson even though his car was, indeed, parked outside.

"Do you think he's done a runner?" asked DS Henderson.

"It looks like it," replied DI McColl. "But, why wouldn't he take his car? That would surely be the most obvious way of disappearing."

"But, we could have every Police car looking for it," said Henderson. "Could he have taken someone else's car instead?"

The uniformed officers checked with all the neighbours. Nobody had seen him go and nobody admitted to loaning him another car. The last time anyone had seen him was when he came home from work on Wednesday evening and went into his house. Nobody else had been seen at the house.

While the neighbours were being questioned, McColl and Henderson checked all through the house and found nothing obvious that appeared to connect Wilson with the murders. Cupboards, drawers and wardrobes appeared to be full so it didn't look as if Wilson had fled from his home. They rummaged around and found his car keys, some money but not a wallet, unopened mail and his lap-top which they took with them so that their colleague, the 'Geek' could look into it for anything incriminating. More importantly, they found a recent photograph clearly showing him at a party. There wasn't a copy of any of the newspapers lying around.

When they had finished inside, McColl looked outside and, at the back of the house, was a small, untidy garden. McColl immediately recognised the bright blue plant growing there, from the pictures he'd seen, as the deadly monkshood that had been used to poison Paul Thompson. For some reason, Wilson hadn't bothered to get rid of it.

It looked as if he must have seen his details in the local paper and had grabbed his wallet and fled without taking anything with him, even his own car. A quick check told them that nobody in the area had had their car stolen so their next check was the CCTV pictures from the nearest railway stations in case he had fled by train but he wasn't in any of these. The bus company which operated the routes nearby also used CCTV in their vehicles and the last two days pictures were also gone through but he didn't appear in any of these either.

Where has he gone? And how?

Fourteen

Monday 23rd August 2010

It was just after seven o'clock on the following Monday morning when the Police Station telephone rang. It was answered quickly and a uniformed constable took down the details.

"Ok. We'll be right there."

"What is it?" asked a colleague.

"A man out walking his dog has just found someone hanging from a tree. Next to Kilmardinny Loch."

"What? You mean hanging, as in dead?"

"That's what he said. We'd better tell Sergeant Miller and get over there as soon as we can."

Two police cars drove as fast as they could to the scene. There were many tall trees between the road and the loch which was popular with dog-walkers and joggers. From a large branch, a thick rope had been tied and the body of a man hung lifelessly on the end of it, with his feet about a metre above the ground. A wooden stool lay on its side beneath him. He had a noose around his neck and the obvious impression the Police got was that he'd hanged himself.

The area around the tree was quickly taped off and more Police officers guarded both ends of the path to stop anyone from casually walking past and being met with the horrific sight. Young mothers with prams or buggies, as well as children taking a shortcut to the nearby school, often used the path and they had to be prevented from seeing such a thing.

The Police took several photographs of the body, from all different angles, and several of the ground beneath him where there were many footprints, before cutting him down and removing the rope. His neck had been snapped and his death appeared to have been instant. According to the Police doctor, he appeared to have been dead for about six or seven hours before he was found. The man appeared to be in his mid to late twenties.

He was a thin, fair haired man, dressed casually. They searched his pockets and found a wallet with some cash and a bank card in it. The name on the card was Donald Wilson. They carefully put his mobile phone and his wallet into clear bags for evidence purposes.

The body was taken away to the mortuary and the Police officers began house to house enquiries on both sides of the nearest road. Nobody had seen or heard anything the night before. One man said that he always walked his two golden labradors last thing at night, about half past eleven and that he'd seen nothing unusual when he walked past the tree. Nobody had heard a car arriving and there wasn't an unidentified vehicle left parked on the road.

"We'd better tell DCI McMeekin," said Sergeant Miller. "This appears to be the guy they've been looking for. The appeal that's been in the papers and on television."

When DCI McMeekin was told what had happened and the name of the deceased, he couldn't believe it.

"You must be joking," he said to the Sergeant. "Donald Wilson? Aged about twenty eight? No way! That's the guy we've been looking for since last week. Is it definitely him? Can we get a positive ID? Fingerprints checked with those at the house? Can neighbours identify him?"

140

"We're doing all that," replied Sergeant Miller. "We'll be able to confirm it very shortly."

'Meek' went to the door of his office and spoke to McColl and Henderson who were sitting at their desks in the main office.

"Donald Wilson's been found", he announced.
"Where? Has he been arrested?" asked DI McColl.

"He's been found dead!" replied DCI McMeekin. "Hanging from a tree beside the pathway close to Kilmardinny Loch. A middle-aged man walking his dog first thing this morning found him and called it in. Uniformed officers closed off the scene. It was only when they found a wallet that they got his name. His description matches and they're getting a positive id as quickly as they can."

McColl and Henderson looked at each other. It was not the start to the week that they had imagined.

The BBC Scotland News website had a short story about the hanging.

A 28-year-old man has been found hanged from a tree beside Kilmardinny Loch in Bearsden, East Dunbartonshire.

Emergency services were called to the woodland at about 07:10.

Police Scotland said that they had been looking for this man in connection with five killings in Bearsden in July and it appeared at this time that nobody else was involved.

A post mortem examination will be held in due course and a report will be submitted to the procurator fiscal.

* * * * *

"So, he's decided to hide and then hang himself before we could get to him?" said McColl. "Was there a suicide note on him? How did he get there? Did anyone see him last night?"

"That's a good three miles or so from his home," said DS Henderson. "How did he manage to get there without anyone seeing him?"

"House to house enquiries on the road that leads to the pathway were carried out by uniformed officers before they realised who he was," said 'Meek'. "Nobody saw or heard anything unusual last night and there's no unidentified car sitting there. They'll check a wider area, of course."

"Could he have been hiding in the woods, do you think?" said DS Henderson. "All this time?"

"Seems unlikely," replied DI McColl. "The woods and paths are very busy with dog walkers, joggers and people out for walks. Or, people who take bread to feed the ducks and geese. It wouldn't be a great place for hiding. And, for four nights? Seems unlikely."

"And another thing," said DCI McMeekin. "Where did he get the rope? If he fled his home suddenly, and went into hiding for four nights, where would he get a rope to hang himself? Stolen from a nearby garden? You need to check that out. Or, did he manage to buy it somewhere over the weekend? Where does one go to buy strong rope these days? That's not the kind of thing that folk have lying around, is it? Go and speak with Sergeant Miller. Find out of it was old rope or if it could have been bought recently. If it was, find out where sells it. A DIY store or garden centre near here? Did anyone get seen buying it? Are they on CCTV? Or, was it stolen from a nearby house? Let's get this case closed at last. Good luck!"

McColl and Henderson found out that the rope that hanged Donald Wilson was new looking, so it appeared to have been bought recently. It wasn't stolen from any of the houses, garages or sheds near to Kilmardinny Loch. Only one DIY store sold rope but they told McColl and Henderson that they had no record of anyone buying any recently.

The rope turned out to be 8mm synthetic looking cord but it had been doubled over to take Wilson's weight without snapping.

"Who sells rope like that?" asked DI McColl. "What is it used for?"

"Could it have been bought on-line?" asked DS Henderson. "No pun intended!"

"Let's try searching on Google," suggested DI McColl.

They logged on and began to look for somewhere nearby that stocked and sold that type of rope. There weren't many places that did. They scrolled down through the list.

"Hey! Look at that!" exclaimed DS Henderson as he noticed the name of a stockist in Glasgow city centre. "The Scout Shop in Elmbank Street sells it. Is that a coincidence or what?"

"And you know I don't believe in coincidences," replied DI McColl. "Let's call them up. Read out the number."

DS Henderson did so and DI McColl called them up. The phone was answered after two rings. DI McColl said who he was and asked to speak to the manager. He was called for and, after a moment, he answered.

DI McColl explained what they were looking for and the shop manager said that they stocked books, uniforms and camping equipment. They sold various types of rope to Scout groups for their different makes and sizes of tents.

"That's one of the thickest ones we sell," explained the manager. "Various people, who go camping, buy from us, not just Scout groups, and that rope is usually used on older ex-army tents rather than the modern, family sized tents that use thin ropes. We stock our ropes on drums or reels and sell it by the metre. It gets cut to size depending how much a customer needs."

"Have you sold any recently? asked DI McColl. "We're probably looking for a man who's bought some in the last week or so, but it might be longer ago than that."

"Do you know how much was bought?" asked the manager.

DI McColl tried to estimate how much rope would have been used by Donald Wilson when he decided to take his own life.

"Probably about six to ten metres, I think," said DI McColl.

"I can't tell you right away," said the manager. "Can I check and call you back?"

"Ok. If you can," replied DI McColl. "Let me know as quickly as possible. And, do you know of anywhere else that sells this rope?"

"Yes," replied the manager. "Most of the other camping or outdoor shops will probably have it, too. Shops like Blacks, Millets or Nevisport for instance."

DI McColl thanked him and they quickly looked up the phone numbers for these other city centre stores. Between them, they called them all and repeated their enquiry.

By lunchtime, all the stores had all checked their sales records and contacted the detective with their answers. One had sold some to a leader from a Scout group that they knew well, from the south of the city. The Scout Shop admitted that is was getting rather late in the usual camping season and they didn't sell as much as in the late spring or summer, but they said that they had sold two lots to groups that they did a lot of business with and who were quite well known to them. They hadn't sold any to a man they didn't know, and they'd checked back several months. The detectives got the details of the Scout groups that had bought the rope and then contacted them to ensure that they had bought it for the 'proper' reasons and could account for what they had bought. These leaders were somewhat puzzled by the enquiry, and one even seemed rather hesitant to answer the question, but they were quite adamant that they had all used the rope to replace worn guy ropes on their tents.

"Do you really think that Wilson would go to a lot of trouble to buy the rope?" asked DS Henderson. "If he had suddenly decided to kill himself when his picture appeared in the papers, he wouldn't go trailing all over the city looking for rope would he? Maybe he'd already decided to do this once he'd committed the last of the murders. Or maybe, he just decided to kill himself because he was racked with guilt because he accidentally killed Mrs Campbell as well?"

Fifteen

Early that morning, the Police Pathologist called DCI McMeekin. "I've just finished the post-mortem on Donald Wilson and, as we expected, he was killed by hanging, but there are a few odd things."

"Odd? What do you mean?" asked McMeekin.

"Well, his stomach's completely empty as if he hadn't eaten anything on the day he died, or even on the two days before. And there are minute traces of a sticky substance on his face which is also slightly discoloured. It would suggest that he was gagged for a couple of days. I asked the Forensics team to check his clothing and they found minute traces of the same substance on his lower sleeves and the bottoms of his trouser legs. It looks as if his wrists and ankles were bound together with a strong tape at some point. The same tape must have been used to gag him as well. Perhaps that black gaffer tape or duct tape that you get at DIY stores. You know the stuff I mean?"

"Yes. Of course. So, are you suggesting that it wasn't suicide?" asked 'Meek'.

"It's somewhat unusual but it looks as if his wrists and shins were taped together, and he was gagged, before he was hanged and then the tape must have been removed once he was dead. He could have been held somewhere for a couple of days, gagged, and not given anything to eat or drink. Whoever did it must have removed the tape very carefully, trying not to leave a trace but we've found it."

"This just gets stranger and stranger. Let me know what else you find," said 'Meek' and he hung up the phone.

He shouted out to the main office and asked DI McColl and DS Henderson to come into his office and shut the door behind them.

"You're not going to believe this," he told the two detectives. "I thought we were nearly ready to close this case at long last, but I've just taken a call from the Pathologist doing the post-mortem on Donald Wilson. It's looking likely that he didn't kill himself after all but he might have been murdered. His wrists and legs appear to have been taped together, and he was probably gagged. He might even have been held captive somewhere for a couple of days since there's no trace of him having eaten anything. It now appears possible that he could have been hanged by someone until he was dead and then the tape's been removed to make it look like he hanged himself. It appears to be rather amateurish as if it wasn't planned properly."

McColl and Henderson looked at each other as if they couldn't believe what 'Meek' was saying.

"So, we've got another murderer out there?" said DI McColl. "Possibly a revenge motive, after we've issued Wilson's photo. Someone's got to him before we could find him."

"And they've maybe even held him captive somewhere then taken him to the loch. He'd not eaten anything for over two days, so he might have been too weak to put up much of a struggle. He appears to have been a rather skinny, undernourished individual so a couple of days without eating would make him very weak indeed," said 'Meek'.

"Could he have been hiding somewhere?" asked DS Henderson. "Do you think he could have trusted someone to keep him so we wouldn't find him? And then his co-conspirator's killed him instead of turning him in."

"This just gets more and more confusing every day," said DI McColl. "We have to hope that someone's seen him, somewhere between his house and the loch."

There were no other informative phone calls for the rest of the day so the detectives finished their shift and went home.

Thursday 26th August 2010

Wednesday had been a wasted day with no progress at all but, on Thursday morning, the 'Geek' came to tell them that he'd interrogated Donald Wilson's lap-top. It hadn't been encrypted or password protected and he'd been able to find lots of information but nothing to give them any idea where he might have fled to.

"I found some details about the monkshood plant, his various on-line accounts where he bought the seeds and the syringes he must have used to inject the poison. His Facebook page showed that he'd been checking on John Lindsay and Stephen Moffat. He'd been looking up electronics and gas explosions from the News. There's no doubt. He was definitely your murderer."

"And no clues about where he might have disappeared to?" asked DI McColl. "No hotels or guest houses? Any train or bus times? Even taxi company phone numbers scribbled down?"

"No. Not a thing," replied the 'Geek'. "He's just disappeared."

"What about his friends?" asked DS Henderson. "Are there any indications of anyone he might have been close to? That he might have turned to?"

"Again, nothing. There are hardly any contacts with anyone. He really was a total loner."

"Try his phone records," suggested 'Meek'. "Find out if he spoke to anyone in the days before he was found. We'll try his colleagues."

This proved to be fruitless as Donald Wilson hadn't phoned anyone either from his home phone or his mobile phone for over two weeks. Those calls he had actually made all proved to be mundane, routine things and had no relevance to the enquiry. When questioned, his colleagues all said that he usually kept to himself and he certainly wasn't staying with any of them.

Friday 27th August 2010

The two detectives went into DCI McMeekin's office for their usual morning update – except that there was very little to update that morning.

"So, he was a loner," said DCI McMeekin. "That makes it rather unlikely that he had a co-conspirator, doesn't it? Unless he wasn't the only boy to be abused. What if there was more than one of them. Wilson's the one we were after so he ran to another house to hide."

"But, why was he hanged?" asked DI McColl.

"Perhaps to make it look like he was the only one involved?" said DCI McMeekin. "Suppose he was working with someone else. Another abused boy from the group. Wilson's hidden in his house yet he knows we were after him. He could have killed Wilson, made it look like suicide, hoping to divert us away from him."

"And, we've no idea who he is," said DI McColl. "When the specialists watched all the video recordings that we found at John Lindsay's, were there any with another boy? Or was Donald Wilson the only victim?"

"Apparently, he was the only one," said DCI McMeekin. "From the reports I was given, he was the only one."

"Unless the other leaders had other recordings," suggested DS Henderson. "There could have been some in Roy Campbell's house before it got blown to bits. He was the leader after all, and he was the one who was the ring-leader on the one we saw."

"Which then poses the question," said DCI McMeekin. "If he had a recording in his house, did his wife know about it? Could he have kept it hidden without her knowing? And watched it when she wasn't there?"

"Surely, we don't have to search the rubble looking for it," said DI McColl, dreading the worst. "That could take months. And, even then, we might not find anything."

DS Henderson then piped up with a cheeky suggestion, with a smirk on his face, "Of course, it could be hidden in the villa in Spain. Perhaps we should go and take a look."

"Don't even think about it," retorted 'Meek', realising that Henderson was only trying to wind him up. "You're not getting a free holiday out of it."

He paused for a moment. "Come on, you two. You're not thinking properly. There has to be a motive. Every crime has one. You just have to work out what it was. Who could have wanted Donald Wilson dead? And why?"

"We're getting nowhere. This case is just proving to be the most frustrating one we've ever had to deal with. We need to clear our heads. Perhaps, then, we might come up with something we've not thought of. Go home, the two of you. Take a break from interviewing and looking at photographs over the weekend, but keep thinking. Try to come up with something new and we'll get together on Monday morning."

The two detectives were glad to get a weekend to themselves. *All work and no play makes Jack a dull boy.* The McColls got Lynne's parents to come and watch the boys and John, Lynne, Scott and Suzy went out for the evening. There was a fairly new Spanish restaurant, called Las Ramblas, opened near Bearsden Cross so they'd booked a table. They enjoyed a delicious meal of paella, Spanish tortillas and grills, washed down with a large jug of Sangria. The case wasn't even mentioned.

Sixteen

Monday 30th August 2010

Refreshed after their weekend, the detectives were ready for a new week. They got coffees and got together in DCI McMeekin's office. They discussed and considered all the facts they knew, and then DI McColl suggested, "There's one person I can think of who could have wanted Donald Wilson dead. And that's Christine Moffat!"

"What?" said DS Henderson. "That's a ridiculous suggestion. How could she?"

"Unless there's someone else involved that we don't know about," replied DI McColl. "She's one person with a huge motive. Wilson killed her husband. Left her distraught. I've seen lesser motives than that before."

"But, how could she get to Wilson before we did?" asked DCI McMeekin. "And then hide him over the weekend, tie him up and hang him? Without a struggle? Ok, he perhaps wasn't the tallest, strongest individual. But, that's not realistic is it?"

"Unless she had help," suggested DS Henderson. "One of his, or her, parents, perhaps? Could they have helped her?"

"We met his mother when we went to the house," said DI McColl. "And we saw all the parents coming out of his funeral. They all looked shattered. None of them looked capable of anything like this."

"And it still doesn't answer the rope question," said 'Meek'. "Where did that come from? You've looked for likely suppliers and none of them have sold any to a stranger. So, unless you can come up with another place that sells it – and who sold it to anyone in the Moffat family – that looks rather unlikely, wouldn't you say?"

"Wait a minute," exclaimed DI McColl. "We asked the shops if a man had bought rope, thinking it was bought by Wilson. They all said no. We didn't ask about a woman, did we?"

"You're right!" said 'Meek'. "Get back onto them and ask."

The first call was to the Scout Shop in Elmbank Street. The person who answered the phone put his hand over the receiver as he asked his colleagues. One of them said that he had indeed sold ten metres of rope to a woman on Friday afternoon, the week before. He thought he recognised her. She might have bought stuff before, or perhaps she worked nearby and he'd noticed her passing by, going to or from her work. He described her as tall, attractive with short, light brown hair and very well-dressed. Perhaps aged about thirty. He didn't see her as a Scout or Cub leader somehow.

"It does sound awfully like Christine Moffat," said McColl. "Do we know where she works? Is it near Elmbank Street? Could she have gone there during her lunchtime or after work?"

"No," said 'Meek'. "We don't know what she does or where she works. Go and speak to her and find out if she bought the rope from the Scout Shop. If she does work nearby, that would explain why the staff there knew her. She wasn't married to Stephen back when he was a Scout leader so she probably wouldn't have gone to the shop on his behalf. But, they might recognise her if she passes the shop every day on her way to her work. We haven't even got a picture of her that we could show to the people in the shop, so go and find out what you can. Bring her in here if you think it's necessary or appropriate."

154

DI McColl and DS Henderson left DCI McMeekin's office and walked out to the rear of the Police station to the car park. They drove to Christine Moffat's house and saw that there was a car in the driveway. They parked, walked up to the front door and rang the doorbell.

Nobody answered. They looked in the front window and could see that the house appeared to be unoccupied. They went to the house next door and the neighbour, who opened the door, told them that the car was Stephen's and that Christine hadn't got round to selling it yet. He also told them that Christine worked as a solicitor in an office somewhere in Dumbarton. She had only gone back to work the previous week and had already got back into the routine of working fairly long hours.

McColl and Henderson went back to their car and called DCI McMeekin to tell him what they'd been told. He told them to drive down to Dumbarton and that someone would call them with the address of the solicitor's while they were on the way there.
They found the address, parked outside and went in the front door to the reception desk. They explained to the girl at the desk who they were and asked if they could speak to Christine Moffat. The girl invited them to take a seat while she called Christine. She was in a meeting with a client but she said she wouldn't be long if they didn't mind waiting.

After five minutes, a door opened and Christine Moffat walked into the reception area. She recognised McColl and Henderson at once.

"Hello," she said quietly. "What is it? Have you arrested Stephen's murderer yet? Have you got some news for me?"

"Not quite," said DI McColl. "There have been some developments, but we need to ask you a couple of questions. Is there somewhere private we can talk?"

Christine asked the girl at the desk if there was a spare meeting room available that they could use. She checked her list and said that there was. Christine took the two detectives through to it and they all sat down. She asked if they wanted a tea or coffee but they both refused.

"You've got me a bit confused," she said. "What are you wanting to ask?"

"First of all," said DI McColl. "Can we ask you .. is this your normal place of work? Are you ever up in the centre of Glasgow?"

Christine looked utterly confused. "I work here," she answered. "Unless I have to go to a client's or to court. But I've not been into Glasgow for months. I've been off work for ages. We were away on holiday and then I was allowed a lot of time off. You know why. But, why do you need to know?"

"I will explain," said DI McColl. "But I have to ask .. do you ever go to the Scout supplies shop in Embank Street, near Charing Cross in Glasgow?"

Christine looked even more puzzled. "No," she replied. "I think I know where it is but I've never been there. Stephen stopped all his involvement with the Scouts years ago. Before we even started to go out. But, I still don't understand."

"How about Thursday or Friday? The 19th or 20th? Were you in Glasgow on those days?"

Christine thought for a moment, still looking completely baffled. "No", she said. "I was in long meetings here on both those days. But, I really don't understand. What are you asking me for?"

DI McColl had to explain. "We found out the identity of the man responsible for Stephen's accident, as well as the deaths of Paul

Thompson, the Campbells and John Lindsay. There was an appeal for information in the papers and on the News last week. The guy just simply disappeared, and we couldn't find out where he was. We assumed he'd seen his picture in the media and had gone into hiding, but then he was found hanged at Kilmardinny Loch last Monday morning."

Christine Moffat gasped. "I heard something about that," she said. "Someone in here was talking about it. But, I still don't get it."

DI McColl went on, "He didn't hang himself. Someone else killed him and tried to make it look like he'd hanged himself. It looks like he was tied up, gagged and held somewhere over the weekend before being hanged."

Christine Moffat sat and listened. She was visibly shocked by what she heard.

"I'm really sorry," continued DI McColl. "But, you are one of the few people who actually have a motive for wanting him dead."

By now, Christine was horrified. "You really thought I might have been responsible?"

"It's not our fault, but we do have to rule out all possibilities. As I said, I'm really sorry."

Christine had started to sob. "I can't believe it. What kind of person do you think I am? Do you not think I've been through enough? I've only just managed to come back to work. I've no idea how I'm ever going to get on with things. My whole life's been ruined, and that guy can rot in hell for what he did as far as I'm concerned but there's no way I could ever do anything like what you are suggesting!"

When she'd recovered her composure, Christine told them the name of a colleague who could confirm that she had been in meetings on Thursday and Friday exactly as she had said. They invited her into the meeting room and she verified Christine's alibi.

Christine was unable to think of anyone else who could have been involved or who might have had a motive. They thanked her for her help and, once again, apologised for upsetting her. As they said, they were only doing their job.

They left the solicitor's, went back to their car and phoned DCI McMeekin.

"It wasn't her," explained DI McColl. "She had an alibi for the Thursday and the Friday. She was in meetings in Dumbarton for the whole of those days."

"So, if it wasn't her, who the hell was it? Every time we seem to have a positive lead, it turns into a dead end. That means there's still someone out there who killed Donald Wilson and we haven't a clue who it could be."

'Meek' paused for a moment. "Alright you two. Come back here and we'll go right back through everything. Names and details. Right from the very start. There must be something that we've all missed."

They all had a quick lunch and then took all their case files and notes into an Incident Room and laid everything out on the table in close to chronological order. They spent the entire afternoon reading through all the statements they had, all the interview notes from their discussions with all the ex-members, and the evidence that they'd gathered. They drew up a new timescale on a whiteboard on the wall, with names and places. It was getting late and they decided to finish and then resume the following morning.

Tuesday 31ˢᵗ August 2010

Once again, the three of them convened in the Incident Room and continued where they had left off the previous evening.

"What it seems to come down to," said DCI McMeekin. "Is that Donald Wilson has been murdered by someone who got to him before we did. The first place to release his name and pictures to the public was The Milngavie and Bearsden Herald on the Wednesday morning, and then the nationals printed it on the Thursday. The same day it was on the television. Wilson disappeared suddenly some time before he was due at work on the Thursday morning, at quarter to nine, but we don't know exactly when. We don't know if his killer saw the pictures in the local paper on Wednesday the 18th or early on Thursday the 19ᵗʰ before Wilson was due at work. Yet there were no signs of a struggle in Wilson's house."

"So, it's possible," said DI McColl. "That someone local saw the pictures and Wilson's name on the Wednesday, knew who he was, and either went to Wilson's house and got invited inside, kidnapped him, and held him somewhere until he was killed – or they've grabbed him when he was outside his house, perhaps even on his way to work, before he's seen any of the papers and realised that we were after him."

"So, according to Wilson's neighbours," said DS Henderson. "The last time he was seen was on Tuesday evening when he got home from work. But nobody saw him leave his house on the Wednesday or Thursday morning – and not take his car? Did anyone see him at any time on Wednesday? Did anyone see him putting out rubbish? Or getting anything out of his car? Did anyone hear a noise during the night? A scuffle perhaps?"

DS Henderson replied that nobody had seen him from the time that he went into his house about eight o'clock on the Tuesday evening until he was found at Kilmardinny Loch the following Monday. And nobody that had been spoken to had heard anything unusual even though some of them said they'd had some of their windows opened during the night since it was quite warm.

"So, how on earth did he get to the loch?" asked 'Meek'. "Did he suddenly become invisible? This is taking too long to sort out. I mean, this is Bearsden and Milngavie we're talking about. These are supposed to be quiet, peaceful residential suburbs yet we've now got six unsolved murders. This isn't gangland Chicago, with Al Capone's mobsters driving about killing people, is it?"

"It's so frustrating," said DI McColl. "Every time we think we're onto something, it turns out to be a dead end. Our suspects turn out to have perfect alibis or else they turn up dead! We don't really know how big this is. There could be lots of other people involved, who we don't even know about yet. There could be dozens of abused boys – or dozens of abusers out there. And they appear to have closed ranks on us. How are we going to find them?"

"We don't even know when Donald Wilson actually disappeared." said DS Henderson. "It could have been Tuesday, Wednesday or even Thursday morning. And we don't know if he went into hiding or if someone else got hold of him without anybody seeing."

The three of them sat in silence for a few moments, not knowing what to say, and then DCI McMeekin broke the silence.

"I think we need to establish a timetable at Donald Wilson's house. Hour by hour. From when he got home on Tuesday the 17th until you got to the house. We need details. Did anybody see him? Or expect to see him, but not? Did a neighbour hear his television on? Did they hear him putting out a bottle or cans in his bin? Was anyone going round the houses on those evenings? Calling at his door? A window cleaner? A charity collector? Anyone? Was he spoken to or was there no reply? Did his curtains open? Were lights put on? He normally left for work just before nine o'clock, a time when other people would be about. Someone taking children to school or nursery. Somebody must know. Go and jog some memories. "

He continued, "Who was the mystery woman at the Scout shop if it wasn't Christine Moffat? Can we get an artist's impression of her? How did she pay for it? Did she use a card? Can we get a name? Or, do need to find out the name of the manufacturer of that rope and get the name and address of every single retailer anywhere within a wider radius. We need to find out who bought a ten metre length of that particular rope recently, and what they then did with it. The answer's out there. We just need to find it."

By "we", 'Meek' once again meant McColl and Henderson. "Donkey work" was the best expression to describe what they were being asked to do. Wearing out shoe leather was the old way of describing it.

The two of them stood up and went back to their desks to plan out a strategy of what to try first.

"Let's go to the Scout shop first," said DI McColl. "That's our best bet if we can find out who the woman was. Then, we should go to Wilson's house tomorrow morning around nine o'clock. We should assume that the same people will be going about their business at the same time as the days he disappeared. We need to ask them all if they saw anything unusual or if they actually saw Wilson heading off somewhere."

The two of them drove into the city centre and into the car park of the Police Headquarters in Pitt Street, conveniently located just two streets away from the Scout shop. They grabbed a quick bite to eat and then walked round to Elmbank Street to the shop. They met the manager and introduced themselves.

DI McColl said, "We've spoken a couple of times about who purchased ten metres of 8mm synthetic rope, probably on Friday the 20th, and one of your staff, who we hope is on duty today, sold a length of it to a woman that day. There was a comment that he might have recognised her from somewhere. A regular customer perhaps or someone that he's seen walking to a place of work near here. Perhaps coming out of Charing Cross station or the multi-storey car park just up the road."

The manager answered, "Yes. That was Terry who sold it. He's here today."

He called to a young man who had just finished serving a customer at the till, and asked him to come over. The detectives introduced themselves and said again why they were there.

"Yes," said Terry. "I remember selling this to a woman just before the weekend. Friday is usually our busiest day but I do remember this. She was very well dressed as if she's some sort of executive or a lawyer or something like that. She looked a bit too posh to be a Scout leader somehow, or so I thought. And she was very specific about the rope she was wanting and she asked me to help cut it for her."

"And you thought you recognised her?" asked DI McColl. "Did she buy stuff here before? Or do you see her walking down the road as if she works near here?"

"I thought I did," replied Terry. "But I could have been mistaken. I'm usually quite good with faces but there are hundreds and hundreds of people who walk past here every day."

"Can you remember how she paid for it?" asked DS Henderson.

"Well, that rope's less than a pound per metre. I'm pretty sure she just paid cash for it."

162

"So there's no way of tracing her?" asked DI McColl.

"Not from here," replied the manager.

"Ok. Time for Plan B," said DI McColl. "If you could sit with a Police artist, to see if you can come up with a likeness of her, we can get a search for her. Do you think you could remember her enough to do that?"

"I think so," said Terry.

They made arrangements for the artist to come round to the Scout shop from the Glasgow Headquarters in Pitt Street.

"In the meantime," said DI McColl. "It wouldn't do any harm to keep your eyes open in case she is someone who walks past here going to work every day. Let us know what time she goes past and we can arrange to have her picked up for questioning. Can you do that?"

The manager and Terry agreed to do all they could to help the two detectives. McColl and Henderson thanked them for their time and their assistance and went back round to the Police car park to collect their car. They drove out of the city centre back to Milngavie before the afternoon rush got started.

"There's not much else we can do this afternoon," said DI McColl. "We'll start early and go and sit in the car outside Wilson's house tomorrow morning. We'll stop every passer-by and ask if they were about at the same time last Wednesday or Thursday."

* * * * *

When John McColl got home, his wife Lynne could see that he was looking very frustrated. He took off his jacket and hung it up, before sitting in his favourite chair and asking the boys how school had been. There was a mixed response. Gregor said he'd had a very good day, and had been selected to play for the school football team that Saturday morning.

"Can you take me, Dad?" he begged. "Mr Muir says it's going to be a very hard game. The other team were champions last year. You've got to come. Will you, Dad?"

John McColl smiled. "Of course I'll be there. You sound as if you'll need all the support you can get. What about you Johnny? What sort of day did you have?"

"Alright," said Johnny. "Except for Chemistry. I hate that! And I hate Mr Robertson. Everyone at school says that he's gay!"

"You can't go saying that!" said John McColl, feeling slightly uneasy that his young son should be saying such things. He'd only been at senior school for two weeks and John, in his mind, still saw him as being a small boy. His vocabulary had certainly been broadened. "And does that make him a terrible teacher then?"
"That's what everyone says!" replied Johnny. "And he gives us far too much homework!"

"Ah! The real truth at last!" laughed John McColl.

Before they could discuss the teaching disadvantages of being gay, Lynne McColl shouted from the kitchen that their dinner was ready. It was Johnny's turn to get drinks for him and his younger brother and he poured out two large glasses of diluting orange. In the process, he managed to splash cold water from the tap onto the kitchen floor.

"Watch what you're doing!" said his mother, sternly as she pretended to hit him with her serving spoon.

They sat down at the table for dinner and the boys, as usual, asked their father what he'd been doing that day.

"Nothing much," he replied. "Just driving around, asking people questions. It's not all exciting chases or arresting people, you know. We spend more time having meetings or interviewing people who might be able to help us. In fact, at the moment, we just seem to be banging our heads off a brick wall."

The boys were both puzzled by this strange impression. Gregor imagined his father and Scott standing in front of a tall wall and literally banging their heads against it. *What a strange thing to do! How is that going to help them catch someone?*

"Never mind, you two!" said Lynne. "Dad doesn't want to keep thinking about his work when he comes home, does he?" She knew that DI McColl had been spending weeks on this case and kept going down dead ends, getting nowhere. She could read the frustration all over his face.

Seventeen

Wednesday 1ˢᵗ September 2010

The next morning, McColl and Henderson drove to Wilson's house in Hardgate, and waited for the first person to emerge. A middle aged man appeared and was getting into his car when McColl and Henderson approached him and gave him a bit of a fright. He told them that he left his home at the same time every morning but, no, he hadn't seen Donald Wilson last week.

Three other neighbours came out of their houses but none of them had seen Donald Wilson. At a quarter to nine, a front door across the road opened and a young woman came out holding the hands of a nursery age girl and a boy with a schoolbag, who looked about six or seven. The two detectives approached them and, at first, the woman looked frightened at the two men standing at her gate. When they showed her their identification cards and spoke to her, she was still very apprehensive. Like the others, she had to tell them that she hadn't seen Donald Wilson or anything out of the ordinary the previous week.

She was about to hurry on, obviously aware of the time and that she needed to get her children to their school and nursery, when the boy pulled at her sleeve.

"What is it?" she demanded. "We're in a hurry, don't you know!"

The boy muttered something to his mother, but she immediately told him to stop wasting time with his silly nonsense. He pulled her sleeve again and she was getting angry.

"Don't be daft!" she admonished him. "You didn't see anything of the sort! Now, come on!"

DS Henderson stooped down beside the boy. "Did you see something? Did you see Mr Wilson from across the road?"

The boy wanted desperately to tell them but he realised that his mother was getting rather angry and harassed.

"It's ok. You can tell us," said DS Henderson. "Did you see something?"

"Yes!" he replied. "I did. Last Wednesday when we were getting ready to go out, I looked out the window and I saw Mr Wilson. He was with two other men."

McColl and Henderson couldn't believe their luck but the woman wasn't believing a word of it. "Don't listen to him," she said. "His head's full of nonsense. He didn't see anything!"

"I did so!" said the boy. "The two men grabbed him and pushed him into the boot of their car. Then they drove away quickly, just like something out of a film."

"Did you know who they were?" asked DS Henderson.

"No. They just came up behind him and shoved him into the car."

"Oh, come on Andrew", said the woman. "That's just ridiculous. Now would you hurry up or we're going to be late!"

DI McColl tried to pacify the woman. "We're desperate for information. We need any help we can get. If your son did see something, we need to know about it. It's very important." He turned back to the boy more in hope than anything else, and asked, "Do you know what kind of car it was? Or what colour?"

"Of course I do. I'm an expert on cars!" he replied. "It was a black Vauxhall Astra. The same kind as Uncle Peter's got. The registration number was something 07 SSN, and it had a round sticker on the back."

McColl and Henderson were amazed. Could this actually be the breakthrough they were looking for?

"Which way did they go?"

"That way", said the boy, pointing in the Bearsden direction.

"Was there anybody else about? Any other neightbours?"

"No. I didn't see anyone else."

McColl and Henderson took a note of the boys' name and address, thanked him and said they would look into it. Then they offered the woman and her children a lift to the school and nursery, which she gratefully accepted as they were now already late. Needless to say, they didn't have child seats in the car but the children put on their seatbelts and it was a relatively short distance anyway. Andrew was thrilled to bits. Being taken to school in a police car. It didn't get any better than that. "Can you put on the blue flashing light?"

"We're not supposed to unless it's a real emergency," smiled DI McColl "But, just wait."

When they got to the school, they drove into the staff car park. Just across from it, there were a lot of children milling about with teachers shepherding them in the doors. McColl winked at Henderson and he switched on the blue light and siren. Everyone looked round to see what was going on and they were all stunned to see Andrew Donachie climbing out of the back door and waving goodbye to the two detectives. *How does he manage to get a Police escort to school?*

"Did you really have to do that," said the mother. "I think we've had quite enough excitement for one day!" The two detectives smiled and then drove her back home. DI McColl gave her his card and asked her to contact him if Andrew remembered anything else.

When they got back to the Police Station, they immediately started a wide search for any vehicles matching the description Andrew had given them. Within half an hour, they had two vehicles within the East Dunbartonshire area which matched Andrew's description. They immediately told DCI McMeekin as they headed out the door to go to the two registered addresses they got from their database.

When they got to the first house in Westerton, a leafy garden suburb between Bearsden and the west of Glasgow, the black Astra was parked outside. According to the Police database, the registered owner was a Mr Mark Livingstone. There was no sign of any sticker on the back. They rang the doorbell of the house and waited. An elderly man answered it. He looked about seventy, was white haired, and walked with a stick. He confirmed that he was Mr Daly and he owned the car but said that he hardly ever used it. He was thinking of selling it to that company that advertised on television that they bought any car for a good price. McColl and Henderson apologised for disturbing him and wished him luck with selling the car.

Then they drove to the second address. It was a semi-detached house in the outskirts of Milngavie. The car was parked in the driveway and it had a round white sticker inside the back window, just as Andrew had described. The owner was registered as Mr Jack Daly.

"Well, I'll be …" said DI McColl. "Look at that!"

On the inside of the rear window was a sticker displaying the name of the Scout's Outdoor Centre at Auchengillan, in the countryside between Bearsden and Drymen. The car owner had a connection with the Scouts.

DI McColl nervously pushed the doorbell. Nobody answered so they looked in the front window. The house appeared to be empty so they had a look around. At the rear of the house was a small shed and, strangely, the two small windows on the side were blacked out. They tried the next-door neighbour's front door instead.

An older woman answered and told them that Mr Daly would be at his work but he normally got home about six o'clock. Crucially, she confirmed that Mr Daly was actively involved with the Scouts. "I think he runs a group somewhere in Milngavie." She told them that he was in his late forties and lived alone. "I think he got divorced about ten years ago."

"Do you know where he works?" asked DI McColl.

The woman apologised that she didn't know where Daly worked or, even, what he did. One or two of his neighbours were at home and McColl and Henderson spoke to them all. The image that they were building up was of a loner who hardly spoke to any of his neighbours. They saw him going out some evenings and they were aware that he was a Scout leader although they weren't exactly sure where.

McColl and Henderson were sure that Jack Daly was involved in the disappearance of Donald Wilson. They thought that he might even have been tied up and hidden in Daly's shed. They phoned DCI McMeekin and told him what they had discovered. At his suggestion, a search warrant was arranged for Daly's house and shed, which would allow them to force entry into the house to look for any evidence They could seize his computer or lap-top, and check the shed for any evidence that Donald Wilson had been kept there against his will.

The inside of the shed was empty apart from a garden chair, some tools and a thick roll of gaffer tape. The arms of the chair had some traces of a sticky residue which the detectives assumed was from the tape as if someone had had their wrists taped to the chair. Had Donald Wilson been ambushed, bundled into the boot of the car by Daly and an accomplice, and then taped to the garden chair in the shed for three or four days with no food or drink? And then, had Daly and the same accomplice taken Wilson to Kilmardinny Loch on the Sunday night, when he'd been too weak to resist, and then hanged him until he was dead and removed the sticky tape from his wrists, ankles and mouth? It certainly appeared that that was what had happened.

Had Jack Daly been involved in the same sordid abuse as Roy Campbell and his staff? Was he part of some anonymous paedophile gang? Had he seen the appeal for information about Donald Wilson and then decided to get to him before the Police found him? How had he known where Wilson lived? How had he found out about Wilson before anyone else? There were so many unanswered questions.

Eighteen

The two detectives and two uniformed officers were waiting for Jack Daly when he arrived home from work at six o'clock. He was completely surprised when they confronted and arrested him. He was sure that no-one had seen him either at Wilson's home or at Kilmardinny Loch and, in his own mind, he was convinced that he had 'got away with it'.

He was taken straight to Milngavie Police Station where he was duly processed by having his fingerprints and photograph taken as well as a mouth swab for a DNA test. All his personal belongings were taken from him by the sergeant on duty. He remained absolutely silent, as was his right to do so, unable to comprehend what was happening to him. He had never been arrested before and the whole experience was alien to him. He knew that he had committed a major crime but he certainly did not expect to be pounced on by several Police officers when he walked home to his house. He was now trying to decide what he was going to do next.

While he was being processed, his lap-top was being investigated by the 'Geek'. A series of disgusting images was found including the video clip of Donald Wilson being abused at the Scout camp seven years ago.

DI McColl and DS Henderson quickly phoned their homes to say that there had been a major breakthrough in the case, that they were beginning to think would never be solved, and that they wouldn't be home for their dinners until much later.

A solicitor was arranged for Jack Daly and he quickly briefed his client about what was going to happen that evening.

McColl and Henderson joined them in the Interview Room, while DCI McMeekin watched the proceedings on CCTV on a screen in another room. Daly was wearing handcuffs and he looked like a rabbit caught in a car's headlights.

DI McColl began by explaining that they were investigating the murder of Donald Wilson who had been found hanging beside Kilmardinny Loch on Monday the 23rd of August. Stretching the truth more than a little, he went on say, "A reliable witness saw two men, outside his house on Wednesday the 18th of August, forcing Mr Wilson into a black Vauxhall Astra, matching the registration number and description of your vehicle which we found parked outside your house. We established from your neighbours that you were at work but they couldn't tell us where that was. While we waited for your return, we obtained a search warrant for your house and shed. We found that the windows of your shed had been blacked out and it appeared as if someone had been held there against his will. Our forensic team is currently checking your car and shed for evidence that Donald Wilson was there at some point. What do you have to say about that?"

Daly glanced at his solicitor and then replied, "No comment."

DI McColl went on, "We also found a lap-top inside the house which had a number of indecent pictures stored on it. These included pictures of abuse being carried out on a boy called Donald Wilson at a Scout camp a number of years ago. Have you anything to say about that?"

Once again, Daly declined to say anything.

DI McColl continued, "Can you tell us who the other man was? The man who was with you when you pushed Mr Wilson into the boot of your car?"

"No comment."

Jack Daly's solicitor sat in silence, carefully making notes of everything that was being said.

McColl went on, "Mr Daly, the evidence that we have leads us to believe that you were involved with a gang of paedophiles. You all shared indecent images on your computers or lap-tops. Mr Donald Wilson, when he was a young boy and a member of the Scouts, was the victim of abuse at a Scout summer camp. You have a recording of that on your lap-top. Our evidence also shows that Mr Wilson killed the four Scout leaders, from his own group, who were involved in that abuse. We appealed for information concerning Mr Wilson's current whereabouts, but when we got to his home address, he had disappeared without trace. He was then found hanged, and all the evidence tells us that you, and an unknown accomplice, got to Mr Wilson before us. You bundled him into your car, held him captive in your shed, with his mouth gagged, and then took him to Kilmardinny Loch and hanged him from a tree, attempting to make it look like he had committed suicide. Are you going to admit this?"

Daly realised that he was in it up to his neck but he stoically managed to maintain his silence as his world came crashing down around him.

"Mr Daly, we can charge you with murder, which was obviously planned in advance. With that, and the paedophile charges, you can expect to be sent to prison for a very, very long time."

Daly could do nothing but stare downwards. The harsh reality that he was finished, that the lifestyle he knew and enjoyed was over, made him start to cry. He sat there sobbing, but still he said nothing.

DI McColl and DS Henderson decided to suspend the interview to let Daly speak with his solicitor. They picked up their notes, stood up and left the Interview Room. They went to DCI McMeekin's office to review their notes.

Daly turned to look at his solicitor for a lifeline. What could he do?

Out in the office of the Police Station, the 'Geek' was at work. The Scout group that Jack Daly was the leader of, had a website. On it, all their weekly activities were detailed. There was a page with a history of the Scouts and their group in particular. There was a gallery of photos and there was a calendar of their events. Importantly, there were recent pictures of all the leaders.

Staring back at them were three men, in their late twenties or early thirties. Any one of them could be Daly's accomplice or part of the paedophile gang. All three of them could even be involved in this expanding alliance of evil.

The 'Geek' printed them out and gave them to the two detectives who were now back at their desks. "One of these might be your mystery accomplice," he suggested.

"These are great! We can go and show these to our friend, young Andrew," said DS Henderson. "He might remember seeing one of them."

"Unfortunately, he's only a kid," replied DI McColl. "His evidence is not really that reliable. Anyway, it's getting late now. By the time, we drive to his home, he could be tucked up in bed."

"So, do we lock Daly up?" asked DS Henderson. "He's not saying anything at all, even though the evidence is piling up against him. Perhaps a night in the cells might get him to talk. By tomorrow, we should have the forensic reports from his car and his shed. We could go and speak to Andrew early tomorrow morning and then come in here. What do you think?"

176

DI McColl was inclined to agree. "We'll have a quick word with 'Meek' and put that to him. Then we can see if Daly wants to tell us anything after he's spoken with his solicitor. If not, we can keep him here until tomorrow and try again."

Jack Daly was still not talking so all interviews were suspended for the day and he was led to the cells to be held overnight.

Nineteen

Thursday 2ⁿᵈ September 2010

The next morning was an early start for McColl and Henderson. They arrived at Andrew Donachie's front door at half past eight when his mother was racing against the clock to get Andrew and his sister ready to go out. *Who's that at the door? Don't they know what time it is?*

When Andrew's mother opened the front door and saw DI McColl and DS Henderson standing there, she got a surprise. "Oh, it's you!"

"I know you'll be really busy, Mrs Donachie, but can we just have five minutes with Andrew?" asked DI McColl. "We arrested one of the two men he saw, thanks to his evidence. Something came up last night but we realised it was too late to come to speak to him, so we were hoping we could see him just now."

Andrew was upstairs, brushing his teeth, but the bathroom door was open and he heard everything. Yesterday had been amazing. He'd been the talk of the school following his 'V.I.P.' arrival in the Police car. *And now, they want to see me again!* He hurried down the stairs and the two detectives were now standing in the hall.

"Hi Andrew," said DI McColl. "You were an absolute hero yesterday. We arrested a man based on what you told us."

"Wow! This is amazing!" said Andrew, unable to contain his excitement.

"We've got three photographs which we'd like you to look at, to see if one of them is the other man that you saw."

"Can we get to ride to school in the Police car again?" asked a very thrilled Andrew.

"Sure. Of course!" replied DS Henderson, smiling.

Andrew's mother rolled her eyes with a sense of exasperation. *Oh no! Not again!*

DI McColl showed the three pictures to Andrew. "Look at these really carefully. Do you recognise any of them?"

Andrew looked at the pictures while his mother turned her attention to his sister. He yelped in excitement when he looked at the second picture. "I know him! That's Fraser Martin! He lives over the road!" shouted Andrew, pointing at a house over the road.

"Are you absolutely sure?" asked DI McColl.

"Yes. Definitely!"

"But, why didn't you recognise him at the time? When he was at the car outside?"

"I couldn't see his face. He had his back round this way," replied Andrew. "But, that's definitely him! Mum, come and see this!"

His mother came over and looked at the photograph. "He's right. That's definitely Fraser. He stays over there with his mother. I think he works at the newspaper in Milngavie, or somewhere like that."

"The Milngavie and Bearsden Herald, in Kirkintilloch, you mean?"

"Yes. That's the one," she replied. "He's something to do with the actual printing. He's not a reporter or anything."

McColl and Henderson looked at each other. They were both thinking the same thing.

He could have been preparing to print the paper on the Tuesday night, before it came out on the Wednesday. He'll have seen the picture of Donald Wilson and then he could have called Jack Daly and tipped him off. The two of them could have been lying in wait for Wilson to come out of his house. Then they've bundled him into the car and taken him to Daly's shed. All this before the Herald even came out on the Wednesday morning.

"Right," said McColl. "Let's get over there and see if he's in."

Before they could move, a young voice piped up beside them. "But you said we could go in the Police car again!"

McColl and Henderson realised they had made a promise to your Andrew, but they had to get across the road.

DI McColl quickly turned to Andrew and tried to explain, "Look. It's very urgent. I'll tell you what … we need to go and question Fraser, probably even arrest him, if he's at home. You've been an absolute star, once again. So, what we'll do is arrange for a police car, with flashing lights to come and take you to school every day next week. What about that?"

Andrew looked at his mum who was shaking her head in disbelief. *Good grief! Not more of this?*

Andrew now couldn't wait to get to school to tell his friends this latest development. "That's amazing! Every single day? Really?"

"Yes. Really," replied DI McColl. "We'll get it arranged."

The two detectives excused themselves and Andrew's mother got the children ready to go out the door. Andrew wanted to stay and watch whatever was going on across the road. This was too good to miss as far as he was concerned. But his mother was having none of it. "You've got school to get to, and we're going to be late if you don't get a move on!"

McColl and Henderson hurried across the road to Fraser Martin's house and rang the doorbell. A middle aged woman opened the door and the two detectives introduced themselves. She explained that she was Mrs Martin, Fraser's mother, and that he was at work. "He does shifts. Some of his hours are a bit strange," she told them.

"So, he's at the paper just now?" asked DI McColl.

"Yes," Mrs Martin replied. "He'll be finishing in about an hour."

DI McColl thought for a moment and then explained. "We need to go and see him, but, if we leave, you might phone him and try and warn him. We'll need to get a couple of officers to come and sit here with you to make sure you don't."

"Why? What's he done?" asked Mrs Martin.

"I can't tell you that," explained DI McColl. "But, we need to go and speak to him."

He called 'Meek', told him what had happened, and requested two officers to get to Mrs Martin's address as quickly as possible. He also asked for another car to go straight to the Milngavie and Bearsden Herald's premises at Kirkintilloch to ensure that Fraser Martin didn't leave before McColl and Henderson got there. The nearest available cars were called and they quickly followed their instructions and two younger officers arrived at Mrs Martin's door within five minutes. While McColl and Henderson had been waiting, they asked Mrs Martin for details of Fraser's car and they passed these to the constables on their way to the newspaper.

McColl and Henderson quickly made their way to Kirkintilloch where they met up with the two constables in the waiting car. They instructed them to go round to the back to cover any other exits in case Fraser Martin tried to flee.

The two detectives went in the front door to the reception area, showed their identification cards to the receptionist, who was more than taken aback, and asked that Fraser Martin was called to the reception. "Call him and tell him there's been a package delivered here for him," they suggested. The girl did so and McColl and Henderson waited for him to arrive.

A moment later, a young man, matching the photograph they had, opened a door and casually walked into the reception area. He headed for the desk and began to ask the receptionist about his parcel when the two detectives approached him. He looked completely surprised when they introduced themselves to him and said that they wanted to ask him about an incident outside his home, the previous Wednesday morning as he had been identified by a witness as being one of two men who had bundled Donald Wilson into the back of a car.

The colour suddenly drained from Fraser Martin's face as he realised what was happening and he knew right away that there was no way out. The girl at the reception desk had been listening to every word and sat behind her desk looking shocked.

McColl began to say, "You need to come with us to the Police Station ..." when Fraser Martin immediately began talking rapidly. "It was Jack Daly! He made me do it! It's all his fault! He killed him! I didn't do it!"

"Whoa!" said DI McColl. "Just a minute! We're arresting you on a charge of being involved in the abduction of Donald Wilson and the possible involvement in his murder. We're taking you to the Police Station to interview you. You do, of course, have the right to remain silent so you don't actually have to say anything. And you are entitled to have a solicitor present while we question you. That solicitor will give you private advice on what you should tell us. I'm not having this investigation ruined by you speaking out of turn and us using that evidence and then some whizz-kid lawyer throwing it out of court because we didn't advise you of your legal rights. Do you understand?"

Fraser Martin mumbled that he understood and the two detectives led him out to their car. The receptionist was still open-mouthed and was trying to decide who to call first – a senior manager to tell him what had just happened, or her best friend to describe the amazing thing she had just seen. *This is like, wow, something off the TV!*

As they drove to Milngavie to the Police Station, Fraser Martin sat in the rear of the car and just stared into space. A few minutes ago, he had been going about his work, getting ready to finish his shift and go home, trying to concentrate on what he was doing, and trying to put the events of the past week into the back of his mind. Jack Daly had told him, quite adamantly, that he would not be caught and would not get into any kind of trouble, and yet here he was sitting, hand-cuffed in the back of a police car, worrying what his mother and his colleagues would say.

DS Henderson drove and DI McColl contacted the two constables who were with Mrs Martin. He told them to tell her that Fraser had been arrested and was being taken to Milngavie Police Station for questioning. She was now unable to contact him so the constables were able to leave her house.

Twenty

Fraser Martin was led into the Police Station and, like Jack Daly, he had his fingerprints, a photograph and a DNA swab taken. He was searched and his personal belongings were taken from him. His wallet, some loose change, his phone, car keys and wristwatch were all placed in a clear plastic bag by the sergeant at the desk, and he was taken to a custody cell.

DI McColl advised him fully of his rights and confirmed the charges against him. He was told that he had the right to a solicitor and, since he had never had any dealings with one, the Police's duty solicitor was arranged to be present. He was also told that he was allowed to tell someone where he was but he decided against calling his mother.

The solicitor arrived, was shown the charge sheet, and met briefly, in the Interview Room with Fraser Martin to tell him what was about to happen. They were then joined by DI McColl and DS Henderson, with 'Meek' watching on CCTV. Henderson switched on the recording device and took notes as DI McColl began the interview.

"Mr Martin," he began. "You are charged that, on Wednesday 18th August 2010, you helped Jack Daly to abduct Mr Donald Wilson by bundling him into the boot of Daly's car. You then took Mr Wilson to Jack Daly's home where you and Mr Daly gagged him and bound him to a garden chair in Mr Daly's shed. Mr Wilson was held there until the night of Sunday 22nd August 2010 when he was taken to the woods beside Kilmardinny Loch where he was hanged from a tree."

The solicitor noted all this down as Fraser Martin sat, staring at the floor beneath him.

DI McColl continued, "Mr Martin do you admit to being involved in the abduction of Donald Wilson?"

Fraser Martin raised his head, took a deep breath and began to speak, "It was all Mr Daly. He made me do it. I didn't want to."

DI McColl interrupted, "We know about his involvement. But what exactly are you saying that he made you do?"

"He knew all about the old Scout leaders and he said that he guessed what was going on. He saw that they'd all been killed and he knew someone was responsible for it. But he said that he didn't know who it was but he had a pretty good idea."

"How did he find out that Donald Wilson was involved in the deaths of the Scout leaders?"

"Mr Daly always said that he was smarter than them. He knew what they'd been up to, years ago. They all tried to get me into it. He showed me the video and some of his pictures but I said I wanted nothing to do with them. He knew that Donald Wilson was the boy who got abused and he made sure that he kept an eye on him, even after all these years. Roy Campbell and the three others obviously didn't so they didn't watch their backs. They just pretended it hadn't happened and got on with their lives, never thinking that it would catch up with them one day."

"So, you knew that the four leaders from the 130th Bearsden Scout group were all paedophiles? You knew that they'd abused that boy at the camp all those years ago?"

"Yes. From what Mr Daly told me, they all shared the video. It was e-mailed to lots of other paedophiles and they all exchanged secret photos and video clips. They'd been doing it for years. When the Scout group stopped meeting, they didn't have access to their own boys any more so they got stuff from other people."

"And Mr Daly was part of this group?"

"Yes. He was."

"Did he ever abuse any of the boys in his own Scout group?"

"No. I don't think so. I don't know. He might have done. He never said."

"What about any of the other leaders in your group? Were any of them in on this?"

"I don't know. I've no idea."

DI McColl continued, "So, you're saying that there was this paedophile gang, who abused that boy and then shared the video with others. But, two of them were married – Roy Campbell and Stephen Moffat. Did their wives know anything about this?"

"No. They somehow kept it all secret. Roy Campbell and John Lindsay were the worst two. I think the others stopped looking at that stuff years ago but those two kept sharing pictures and stuff."

"When did you hear about the deaths of these men?"

"I saw it on the News and in the papers. Mr Daly saw them too and he guessed what was happening but he didn't know which of the boys it was, or even if it actually was one of them."

"Are you saying that there were other boys abused in the Scout group?"

"Yes. I think they targeted a boy every year at the camp."

"Did they abuse any of the boys at their Friday night meetings?"

"I don't think so. When they were at the camp, the boys were trapped there. They couldn't tell anyone. The staff could get them at night. If they were all frightened, it was just put down to them being homesick or missing their mothers. They were too scared to say anything."

"So, Mr Daly believed that a victim from years ago, who was now older, was getting back at the leaders?"

"That's exactly it. He was worried that whoever was doing it would get caught and tell everyone what had been going on. He was terrified of being exposed as a paedophile, and of going to jail. He knew I worked at the paper so he told me to keep my eyes and ears open in case there was suddenly a name being revealed."

"So, when you were printing the paper on the night of ..." said DI McColl as he checked his notes. "...Tuesday the 17th of August, you saw the pictures of the unidentified Donald Wilson and you recognised him because he lived across the road from you."

"That's right," replied Fraser Martin. "I knew right away who it was so I phoned Mr Daly. He came to my house and we waited in the car until we saw Donald coming out of his house."

"And then you abducted him?"

"Yes. He walked up behind Mr Daly's car and we just shoved him into the boot and drove away. Mr Daly drove to a deserted spot and we got out and opened the boot. Donald was screaming, terrified, but there was no-one to hear. He recognised me right away but he was just terrified."

"Then what happened?"

"Mr Daly shouted at him, and told him that the Police were after him. He made him confess to killing the four leaders and then we both taped his hands together, and his feet and gagged him. He tried to struggle but he was too petrified to resist."

"And then you took him to Mr Daly's house?"

"No. It was broad daylight so we couldn't take him out of the car in case anybody saw us. Mr Daly phoned his work and said he wouldn't be in that day as he was feeling sick. We stayed there, out of the road, for a few hours so that nobody would see or hear us. That night, when it was dark, we went to Mr Daly's house and put Donald in the shed. Nobody saw us. We taped him to the seat and then Mr Daly stuck some thick card over the windows. Donald was really scared. He was trembling all the time and his eyes had a look of sheer terror. We left him locked in there and then Mr Daly took me home and told me not to tell anyone."
"So, you just left him there for four days with no food or water?"

Fraser Martin hung his head. "Yes. That was Mr Daly's plan. To make him far too weak to struggle. I don't know if Mr Daly checked on him at night or anything. He might have."

"Then, what happened on the Sunday night? The 22nd of August?"

"It was late at night and I drove to Mr Daly's house. We got Donald out of the shed. He was really groggy and we had to carry him to the car. We put him in the boot again and Mr Daly got a stool and we drove to Kilmardinny Loch. I thought at first that he was going to drown him in the loch. He was too weak to have been able to swim. Then Mr Daly got some rope out of a bag and he doubled it up and made a noose."

"Do you know where he got the rope from? Did he go into town to buy it?"

"I don't think so" replied Fraser Martin. "We keep lots of that type of stuff in our store. I think he probably just went and got it from there."

"What happened next?"

Mr Daly fixed the rope to a tree and then I held Donald up on the stool while he put the noose around his neck. He was so weak, he couldn't even struggle."

"And then one of you kicked the stool away?"

"Mr Daly spoke to him and told him that he was murdering scum and could rot in hell for killing the Scout leaders. He really frightened him. Mr Daly told him that he had to pay for what he'd done. He even asked him if he'd rather rot in jail for years. Then he kicked away the stool. Donald dropped down and stopped moving. We watched for a few minutes then Mr Daly took all the sticky tape off his arms, legs and mouth to make it look as if he'd hanged himself. We took one last look and then we drove away as quietly as we could."

DI McColl decided to terminate the interview at that point. The recording device was switched off and Fraser Martin was led back to the custody cell, but he was told that there would possibly be further questions that they would need to ask him. The solicitor spoke to DI McColl, "You can't deny that Mr Martin has certainly provided you with a great deal of genuinely useful incriminating testimony. I sincerely hope that is taken into account when he goes to trial."

DI McColl conceded that Fraser Martin had, indeed, been very useful and, without him, the final pieces of this exasperating jigsaw could never have fitted together. "It's been noted," he said.

McColl and Henderson joined DCI McMeekin in his office.

'Meek' spoke first. "Well done, the pair of you. I think that is what we refer to in the force as 'singing like a canary'. Fraser Martin's testimony is more than enough to convict Jack Daly of pre-meditated murder, and we've also got all the indecent images off his computer. Forensics have finalised their report and Donald Wilson's DNA is all over the boot of Jack Daly's car and in his shed. He could have been the Scout leader that was recognised in the Scout Shop when he bought the rope. The staff said they knew a couple of the buyers as regular customers. He could been one of them, or he may actually have had some of that rope already in his possession. That's not critically important now."

"At last!" said DI McColl. "That, after all the investigations, all the dead-ends, we've finally got this case solved. It's been so frustrating. This case has gone on for far too long, don't you think?"

"Absolutely!" replied 'Meek'. "We've tied up the chain of murders and we should also be able to get evidence against a whole gang of paedophiles as well. When all this becomes public knowledge, who knows, maybe more victims will come forward."

"You don't know whether or not to feel sorry," said DS Henderson. "Donald Wilson suffered that terrible abuse. He lived with it for years, for more than half his life in fact, and he felt unable to tell anyone. And his last days were just cruel. Locked in that shed with no food or water. Possibly with no idea of time. Not knowing what was going to happen to him. And then, to be taken to the woods and hanged. Poor guy."

"But he did kill five people," said DI McColl. "He was a sad individual who planned all those deaths and made three of his victims really suffer. The Campbells, at least, knew nothing."

"So," asked DCI McMeekin. "In the end, is that justice?"

Neither McColl or Henderson answered.

"But, what about the mysterious woman who also bought the rope?" asked DS Henderson.

"Oh, I don't think we need to pursue that line of enquiry now," replied 'Meek. "She can't actually have been involved. What she does with the rope is her own business."

* * * * *

At the formal request of DCI McMeekin and his immediate superiors, the Court seized all the assets of John Lindsay and Paul Thompson (their houses and belongings), Roy and Victoria Campbell (the insurance value of their home as well as the proceeds from the sale of their villa in Spain) and Donald Wilson, who had died without leaving a will, (his house and belongings) and all the money was donated to the charity, Childline, which helps vulnerable or abused children.

Once all the details of the case had become known, two other ex-members of the 130th Bearsden Adventure Scouts came forward and gave statements to the Police, saying that they had also been the subjects of abuse by the four leaders at camps held during previous summers.

A major Police investigation, following the discovery of indecent images and videos found on the confiscated lap-tops, led to the arrest and subsequent convictions of eight other paedophiles. All were given very lengthy jail sentences by the courts.

Christine Moffat could not believe that her husband had been involved in such awful, depraved activities before she met him. Although, the video showed him restraining Donald Wilson to let the other Scout Leaders abuse him, and not actually appearing to be guilty of carrying out any acts of abuse himself, she tried unsuccessfully to clear his name. When that failed, she decided to revert to her own maiden name and to move away from Bearsden in an attempt to start afresh.

* * * * *

John McColl had another very good reason for being satisfied that the case was finally solved, He had promised his younger son, Gregor, that he'd be able to go to watch him playing football for his school team, and he didn't intend to disappoint him. The boys were both old enough to realise that their father often had to work at weekends, and sometimes at short notice, but that didn't lessen their disappointment if he was the only father not standing on the touchline.

Not only that but their mother had told them that Aunt Suzy was coming to visit them that night, and that meant she'd be bringing sweets. *Saturdays just can't get any better!*

Author's Note

My thanks go to my wife, Norma, for thoroughly checking my manuscript with a fine-toothed comb, and for pointing out the few errors in my text. Thanks also go to Chris Jones for his very helpful criticism, guidance and suggestions.

The 130th Bearsden Scout Group does not exist, and never has existed. The names of the leaders and the boys are, of course, entirely fictitious, and they are not based on any real persons whatsoever.

For boys or girls, being a member of a well-run youth organisation, which provides a programme of weekly activities as well as a summer camp, is something I would thoroughly recommend. Friendships made there can last a lifetime, as can all the happy memories of these times spent away from home. Special thanks should be extended to any leader who voluntarily gives of their own time to arrange such a holiday for young people. If the weather is good, a camping holiday in Scotland, is one of the best experiences for anyone.

Gordon Cubie
December 2014

UNPROVABLE

Gordon Cubie

In his debut novel, Scottish writer, Gordon Cubie, tells the story of Alan Gray a man for whom everything is going wrong.

His wife's left him. He's heavily in debt. Someone he hates is about to become his boss and make his life an absolute misery.

Then Alan comes up with a plan for a murder. A clever plan. The Police can catch him easily. They have fingerprints, DNA and witnesses. They know he did it – but they can't prove it.

The trial approaches. Has Alan Gray managed to commit the perfect crime?

Printed in Great Britain
by Amazon.co.uk, Ltd.,
Marston Gate.